m

PUFFIN BOOKS

Mama's Going to Buy You a Mockingbird

Jean Little's many books for young readers include *Kate*, *From Anna* and *Listen for the Singing*. She has received awards not only in her native Canada but also in the U.S. and Europe, and her work has been translated into French, German, Dutch, Danish, Japanese and Braille. Ms Little lives and works in Guelph, Ontario.

Mama's Going to Buy You a Mockingbird

Jean Little

Puffin Books

PUFFIN BOOKS
Published by the Penguin Group
Penguin Books Canada Ltd., 2801 John Street,
Markham, Ontario, Canada L3R 1B4
Penguin Books, 27 Wrights Lane, London W8 5TZ, England
Viking Penguin Inc., 40 West 23rd Street,
New York, New York 10010, USA
Penguin Books Australia Ltd., Ringwood,
Victoria, Australia
Penguin Books (NZ) Ltd., 182-190 Wairau Road,
Auckland 10, New Zealand

Penguin Books Ltd., Registered Offices:
Harmondsworth, Middlesex, England

First published by Penguin Books Canada Limited, 1984
Published in Puffin Books, 1985
Reprinted 1985, 1986 (twice), 1987 (twice), 1988

Manufactured in Canada by Gagne Printing Ltd.

Canadian Cataloguing in Publication Data

Little, Jean, 1932-
Mama's going to buy you a mockingbird
ISBN 0-14-031737-6
I. Title.

PS8523.I87M35 1984   jC813'.54   C84-099006-5
PZ7.L57Ma 1984

For Mark and Sarah deVries
with my love

Acknowledgements

The quote on page 98 is taken from the first sentence of *Kim* by Rudyard Kipling. *Kim* was first published by Macmillan in London in 1929.

The hymn read at Adrian Talbot's funeral on page 119 is "Be Thou My Vision." This was an old Irish poem, circa 8th century. It was translated by Mary E. Byrne in 1905 and versified by Eleanor H. Hull in 1912. It can be found in *The Hymn Book of the Anglican Church of Canada and the United Church of Canada*, published in 1971.

The scripture passage read by Melly at the cottage on page 131 is from Revelations 21: 1 – 5. It is taken from *The New Testament in Modern English*, J.B. Phillips, translator, published in London in 1960 by Geoffrey Bles Ltd.

Tess's song on page 203 is a poem called "The Birds" by Hilaire Belloc, first published by Messrs. Duckworth and Co. I got the words from *An Anthology of Modern Verse*, Methuen's English Classics, 1921. I am told that this poem has been set to music by several composers, among them Benjamin Britten, whose music for it I heard sung by a girl only a little older than Tess.

On page 205 Melly quotes "A Song for Ookpik" from *Nicholas Knock and Other People* by Dennis Lee, published by Macmillan of Canada, a division of Gage Publishing, 1974. Reprinted by permission. All rights reserved.

I want to express my thanks to Shelley Tanaka who has worked with me on this story for years. She not only believed in it; she found a publisher for it and edited it with patience, incisive skill and mounting excitement. Jeremy and I would never have made it without her.

One

"Can I come, too?" Sarah asked.

Jeremy jumped. The dreamy look left his eyes. Lost in his thoughts, he had not known that she was there until she spoke. Now he looked up at her standing on the dock above him.

"No," he said.

"I have my life jacket on."

"No," he repeated, his voice hard.

He gave her no reason for his decision. He knew better. Give Sarah any excuse for an argument and you were asking for trouble. She was like a bulldog; she never gave up. Now, instead of going away, she stayed right where she was and drooped with disappointment. She looked so sad and small that he wanted to hit her.

"You heard me," he told her, stung into speech by her waiting silence. "I said 'No' and I meant it. Do me a favour and scram."

Sarah's lips parted, but if she had thought of answering him back, she stopped herself. He had no business ordering her off the dock, and she knew she could get him into trouble with Aunt Margery by telling on him. She also knew that if she tattled, she would never get to go out in the rowboat with him. Well, not today, anyway. She held her tongue and went on waiting.

Jeremy turned away. Let her stand there forever. He couldn't care less.

Go ahead and bawl, he thought. See how far it gets you. He pushed back his brown hair which badly needed cutting and studied the cloud formations above the cottage. Then he began to whistle as if he had entirely forgotten her presence.

But Sarah Talbot, though she was nearly four years younger than her brother, still knew a few important things about him. One of these was when not to cry. Another was that, tough as he tried to sound, he had a soft heart. She remained visibly hopeful.

Having ignored her for a full minute, Jeremy could not resist darting a glance at her to see how she was taking it. Her head was lowered so that her hair fell forward on either side of her face. She made no sound, not even a whisper of a sigh. Jeremy remembered Dad telling him about a man called Gandhi who had changed the history of India by simply sitting still and waiting for his enemies to give in. At that moment, Jeremy saw why it had worked. Sarah had not begged him or bribed him or threatened him or even tried to explain to him how she was feeling. Yet in some mysterious way, she had put him in the wrong.

Of course, he already knew how she was feeling. She

was lonely, maybe even lonelier than he was. After all, he was older. Dad and Mum told him more and it was easier for him to piece together bits of overheard conversation and make sense out of them.

It was Dad's illness that had changed everything. Mum said that he had been sick for quite awhile before he went for a check-up after school closed at the end of June. Then the doctor had made him go right into the hospital for tests, even though they had already started packing to go to the cottage. The next thing Jeremy knew, Mum was telling Sarah and him that Dad had to have an operation. Aunt Margery was going to take them to the lake so that Mum would be free to visit their father and do all she could to help him to get better fast.

"It's wonderful of Margery to do this," she said. "Otherwise you two would be stuck here in the city with nothing to do but perish from heat prostration."

All their friends were away and it had already been hot in Riverside, so he and Sarah had been glad to go. Dad had had the operation the day after they left. But Jeremy didn't know for sure what had happened. Dad must be better, yet Aunt Margery got upset every time he tried to ask about it. Mum had phoned but never when he and Sarah were in the cottage, and Aunt Margery said it would be no use calling her back because she used a pay phone at the hospital. Finally, last night, he had had a chance to speak with her, but as she handed him the receiver Aunt Margery had hissed, "Don't plague her with questions, Jeremy. She has enough to bear without that." Then Mum herself had sounded so tired and worried that he hadn't been able to ask her about all that he wanted to know.

Well, they'd be here in a couple of weeks. That much he had found out. Till then the trick was to think of other things. It would have been easier if Aunt Margery were different. Not that she wasn't nice to them. It was just that she wasn't . . . well, she wasn't Mum. Mum laughed more and had fewer rules.

Jeremy went back to watching Sarah. Even if she were putting on that mournful look, he could see that underneath it lay real misery. It showed in the hunch of her skinny shoulders and her ducked-down head, in her bitten fingernails, even in the way her toes kept bunching up and then flattening out. He felt sorry for her but he still did not want to be bothered with her. If he could fix things for her it would be different, but he couldn't even fix things for himself.

Irritated at his momentary weakness, he did his best to appear menacing, shifting his weight as though he were about to come after her. Her head jerked up. Her eyes widened a little. But she stood her ground. He liked her toughness. He could beat her up with one hand tied behind him and she knew it, yet she wouldn't run.

"Anyway, I'm not going anywhere." he told her.

Before he had the words out of his mouth, he knew they were a mistake. Dad always said, "Give Sarah a foot and she'll take a leg and an arm as well."

"You've got the paddles hooked into their things," she pointed out, her voice mild, her eyes gleaming. "And you've untied the rope at the back."

"For crying out loud, Sarah," he snapped, "they're not paddles, they're *oars*. And those are oarlocks, you dummy. You don't call it the back of the boat, either. You say the stern."

Straightening her out on so many things all at once made him feel better. Sarah looked properly impressed.

"Oh, yeah," she said. "I guess I forgot."

"You're plenty old enough to remember."

He heard himself sounding like Dad and nearly smiled. In the short silence that followed, Jeremy could see her making up her mind what to try next.

"Why do you have the oars in the oarlocks," she asked, "if you aren't going anywhere? And why . . ."

". . . did I untie the stern?" he finished for her. "Well, sister dear, if it is any of your business, which it isn't, I thought I might want to go somewhere later so I got ready just in case. Satisfied?"

He should have known better.

"If you do go later, can I come?" she said.

He hardened his heart.

"No. I want to go by myself."

"Did Aunt Margery say you could take the boat out?" she asked softly.

Outraged at this veiled threat, he stopped feeling even faintly sorry for her.

"I don't have to ask Aunt Margery and you know it. Last summer Dad said I was old enough to take it out whenever I liked. Buzz off, you little brat. Go play with Paul and quit bothering me."

Instead of departing, Sarah squatted down on the dock so that she was even closer to him.

"I hate Paul!" she said, her voice trembling. "I'm never going to speak to him again. Never ever!"

Jeremy had heard that before. Paul Denver, the only child Sarah's age at their end of the lake, was a whiner, and Jeremy didn't like him any more than she did. He was worse than useless when they played games needing imagination, and yet he could twist the truth so cleverly when he tattled that it was hard to deny what he said even though you knew he was lying.

But now Jeremy realized that something worse than usual must have happened. Sarah wasn't just mad. This particular upset was somehow different.

"What did Paul do?" he asked, keeping his tone matter of fact.

Sarah lifted her head, looked at him and then went back to examining her toes.

"He said that his mother said that Daddy is a very sick man. And she told him that I was a poor little girl and he was supposed to be kind to me no matter how bad I am. He said his mother feels sorry for us."

She spoke in such a low voice that Jeremy could barely understand her, but as her words registered, he felt inside himself her bewilderment and outrage.

"So what did you do?" he asked, knowing that she would not have let that pass.

"I punched him in the stomach and he went bawling to Mrs. Denver and Aunt Margery. He yelled that I hit him and he hadn't done anything to me first. And Aunt Margery . . ."

She choked and Jeremy put his hand up and patted the foot nearest to him.

"Slow down and don't be a bawl-baby like Paul Denver. Now tell me about Aunt Margery."

Sarah had control of herself again.

"She said Paul's younger and smaller than me and she made me say I was sorry."

"I wish I had been there," her brother said, his hands

tightening into fists."I'd have fixed him. Catch me saying 'sorry'!"

Sarah glanced up at him again.

"You would have," she said flatly.

She was right and he knew it. What chance did a kid have when grown-ups took sides with a wart like Paul Denver? But what was Sarah going on about now? He must have missed something.

"Hey, stop talking to your big toe," he said. "I can't hear you when you mumble. Tell me that last part again."

She took a deep breath, raised her chin slightly and repeated herself. "When Paul left, I had a swing and then I went inside to get Fiona. I didn't want Aunt Margery to know I was there. She was busy talking to Paul's mother. So I tiptoed . . ."

She was still squatting there on the dock and, as she spoke, she somehow coiled herself as tightly as a spring with her shadowed face tucked down against her knees. All Jeremy could see of her were her legs and arms and the top of her head, but he noticed she was trembling. If only Mum were here! But she wasn't. He would have to do his best. He stayed where he was and waited.

"I heard them talking. Aunt Margery was telling her that Mum said that the doctor said . . ."

She hesitated. Jeremy felt he would fly apart.

"Yeah, yeah, go *on*," he urged.

". . .the doctor said Daddy had left something too late and now there's only a fifty-fifty chance. Aunt Margery said she had warned them but they wouldn't listen . . . I can't remember exactly. When she saw me, she got really mad. She said I sneaked up. But the door was open. Mum says to knock if the door is shut. Jeremy, what's a fifty-fifty chance?''

For a long moment, Jeremy sat absolutely still. Then he reached out to untie the knot that tethered the bow of the boat and said in an ordinary, everyday voice, ''Get in. I've changed my mind. I'll take you for a row.''

Two

Jeremy's invitation was so unexpected that for a full three seconds Sarah could not take it in. She just stared at him blankly as though her ears were playing tricks. Then, seeing that he meant it, she was transfigured with delight.

"Oh, Jeremy, thanks!" she cried and slid into the boat, landing as lightly as a bird.

She settled on the seat opposite him, making herself at home instantly. He began manoeuvring the boat away from the dock and out into deep water.

Knowing he had to concentrate, Sarah did not talk at first but just sat still, beaming. When he started to pull evenly on both oars, she sang through "Row, Row, Row, Your Boat" a couple of times. Then she studied the surface of the lake.

"It looks as though bits of the sky have fallen into the water and now they're melting," she said.

It did look exactly like that. He nodded and went on rowing. He wanted to put a good big stretch of water between himself and Aunt Margery. He and Sarah would have to go back, of course, but for a few minutes he could put them out of reach of her voice. He wished he could round the point so that she would not be able to see them, either. But Dad had made him promise to stay within sight of the dock unless he were with an adult. They went as far as possible and then turned.

"Go carefully on your hands and knees past me and you can sit in the bow coming back," he told his sister. "Then you can be lookout and tell me if I'm going to run into any rocks."

As Sarah inched past him, he smiled to himself. This old flat-bottomed boat was so heavy that he thought Sarah's weight plus his own would not be enough to tip it even if they were trying their hardest. It made sense, though, always to be careful in boats and he did not hurry her. When she was safely perched in the bow, he began to row again, taking his time. He remembered how he had loved riding up there when he was her age. You felt powerful and peaceful at the same moment. It seemed that the water, the rocky shore and the immense blueness of the sky itself all belonged to you personally. He felt her shift and, without needing to look, he knew she was leaning over the gunwale, trailing her fingertips in the cool water.

"Don't lean out too far," he cautioned,

He knew she wouldn't but he said it anyway. It was like saying, "Don't forget to wish," when someone was all set to blow out birthday candles or like Mum calling, "Get that light out," just after the clock struck nine. It made the moment complete.

"Aunt Margery sees us coming," Sarah said, breaking into his train of thought. "She's waving."

"Are you waving back?"

"No."

He let it pass. Aunt Margery shouldn't have made her apologize to Paul.

"I'll bet she thinks I don't see her," Sarah said. "Jeremy. . ."

Darn, he thought. He braced himself.

"What's a fifty-fifty chance?"

"Dad's been sick," he began, thinking fast. "You know that."

"But what. . .?"

"Do you want me to tell you or not?" he growled. That silenced her. He went on doggedly. "They were saying how worried they were before the operation, I guess. You know he had an operation. I talked to Mum last night myself and she said they were coming up here in a couple of weeks. Dad must be okay if they're letting him leave the hospital to come here, right?"

"Why didn't you wake me up? I wanted to talk to Mummy!" Sarah wailed and burst into tears.

"Pipe down. Aunt Margery will hear you," he shouted over her howling. "Mum said not to wake you and I didn't tell you this morning because I knew you'd bawl just the way you're doing right this second. Dry up! I hardly said ten words to her myself. Heck, they'll be here in two weeks!"

"How many days are in two weeks?" she asked through her sniffling.

"Not many. Mum said to do what Aunt Margery tells us and to help her as much as we can."

Sarah cheered up a little. The familiar sound of those

orders brought her mother closer. Maybe two weeks would pass.

"But I want her *now!*" she protested, giving one last hiccupy sob.

"So who doesn't?" Jeremy retorted.

He wished he could stop worrying as easily as she seemed to have done. But the strain in his mother's voice had betrayed the fact that Dad was not all better the way they had hoped.

"Aunt Margery's coming down to grab the rope," Sarah said.

"Throw it to her," he replied.

Then, as the boat and dock came together, he turned his head and smiled at his aunt.

"How about having a cookout tonight, Aunt Margery? Sarah and I can get the wood and I'm good at building a fire."

She looked surprised.

"Thanks, but I have spaghetti and meatballs planned."

"Oh, boy, I love spaghetti!" Sarah cried.

She scrambled out of the boat. Jeremy tied it securely and then followed her. He took off his life jacket but Sarah, as usual, had got the ties on hers in a tight knot. Aunt Margery reached out to undo it for her. Sarah backed away. Her bottom lip jutted out.

"I can do it myself," she insisted.

Her aunt shrugged.

"Make sure you put everything away properly, Jeremy, before you leave," she directed as she set out for the cottage.

Jeremy, glimpsing her expression a second before she

turned her back, sighed. Her mouth had been set and her cheeks red. Sarah must have hurt her feelings. Well, he had done his best to be friendly. Aunt Margery had hurt Sarah's feelings, too. Once again he longed for his mother.

He undid Sarah's life jacket and put it with his own underneath the canoe which was upturned near the dock. Then he looked down at his sister.

"She wasn't trying to be mean," he said "Mum says she's not used to children. She doesn't know Paul Denver the way we do. Give her another chance."

He did not wait for her to answer but led the way to the cottage. From just behind him, he heard her voice.

"It's fourteen days, isn't it?" she said softly.

It took him only a split second to understand.

"Yes." Looking over his shoulder, he smiled at her. "We can make it, kid."

"I guess so." She still sounded forlorn.

They walked a few steps in silence. Then he heard her small voice again.

"She puts onions in her meatballs."

"Oh, yuck!"

"Maybe she doesn't, maybe I just made that up," Sarah said quickly. "But I think she does."

Jeremy gazed down at her, a skinny little girl, her chestnut hair blowing slightly, her wide brown eyes too serious.

"I guess, if we try hard, we might survive onions," he said, doing his best to sound strong. "It could be worse. It might be Brussels sprouts."

"Or rhubarb!" Sarah said with a watery smile.

"Don't even suggest such a thing!" he said with a

dramatic shudder. "If there's one thing I can't stand, it's rhubarb in my meatballs."

When she laughed out loud, he felt as though he had won a prize.

Three

It was three weeks and a day before Mum and Dad actually came. Sarah, wild with excitement, woke Jeremy by shouting, "Mummy and Daddy are coming today!" He half opened his eyes, yawned and said in his sleepiest voice, "So what else is new?" Sarah was not fooled. She laughed and went rushing off to tell Aunt Margery the glad tidings.

Ever since Dad had not been well enough to make the long drive a week ago, Jeremy had been afraid to believe that his parents would really arrive. Yet, when no phone call came, he felt within himself a great peace and a singing delight. Soon the lonely days would be over. Soon the summer, with all its joy, would finally begin.

After lunch, Sarah, worn out with waiting, fell asleep on the couch. Aunt Margery curled up with a book. Jeremy left the cottage and climbed a tree. He couldn't see the car from that vantage point but he would be sure to hear it. And it seemed right to perch up there, keeping watch. He felt like a sailor in the crow's nest, looking out for the first sight of land.

Beep. . . beep. . . beep, beep, beep! The car horn sounded as they crested the last hill.

Jeremy risked life and limb as he slithered to the ground in one long slide. Then he went tearing down the lane to meet them. Behind him he heard the screen door bang shut as Sarah slammed out of the cottage. She dashed after him, screaming, ''Wait! Wait for me!'' He knew he should slow down and let her catch up to him but he couldn't. His feet skimmed over the rough ground. If Mum hadn't put on the brakes, she would have run over him. Too excited to care, he yanked open the rear door and piled into the back seat behind his father.

Sarah, hard on his heels, tried to scramble in also but he was too winded and too crazy with joy to make room for her. She did not waste time yelling at him. Instead she sped around to the other side of the car and clambered in next to him.

Mum and Dad undid their seatbelts and turned their laughing faces to greet their offspring.

''Who on earth are these hooligans?'' Dad asked. ''Friends of yours, Melly?''

''Oh, Daddy, you know who we are!'' Sarah squealed, rising to the bait as she usually did.

''I do believe it's Henry Huggins and Ramona the Pest,'' Mum said, her eyes loving, ''large as life and twice as natural.''

Jeremy could feel a silly grin stretching across his face till it seemed as though it must touch his ears. Now, at last, they were all together. He felt as though he had been waiting for this moment for years and years.

"Welcome, strangers," Aunt Margery called, coming toward the car.

Mum stuck her head out the window.

"Out of the way, lady, till I get properly parked," she said. "Then I'll get out and hug you. I'm so relieved to find you still in one piece."

Aunt Margery laughed and moved back while Mum parked the car.

"All ashore who are going ashore." Then she said quickly to Dad, "You wait, Adrian, until I can get around and give you a boost."

"I can manage," Dad said. There was an edge to his voice that Jeremy had not heard before. Sarah had jumped out of the car already but Jeremy paused, watching his father fumble with the door handle. Why was Dad so slow? Now he had opened the door and was turning to get out of the car, but it seemed as though he were caught in slow motion, like the replays on TV. Aunt Margery was stepping forward but before she could help, Mum had slipped around her and had given Dad a neat hoist to get him to his feet. He steadied himself with one hand and gave a sheepish laugh.

"I'm still as weak as a kitten, Margery," he told his sister.

"Well, who wouldn't be weak after coming through all you have done in the last month," she said. Her voice sounded husky. Jeremy knew how she felt. He had a lump in his own throat. Dad had always been so strong.

Sarah was now pushed close against Mum, clinging to her as though she planned never to let her go again. Dad was holding on to Mum's elbow. Father, mother and child faced about all together and headed for the cottage. Aunt Margery, following a little behind, snatched a

handkerchief out of her pocket and blew her nose hard.
Jeremy felt abandoned.

He had not expected Dad to look so white and tired.
Mum looked tired, too. Her tan had faded and she had
dark circles under her eyes. But that was different. She
just looked as though she needed a few days' rest. Dad
looked really sick.

"Jeremy," Mum said over her shoulder, "could you
carry in the bags, do you think? And the food? The key
to the trunk is there in the ignition."

Jeremy had to clear his throat before he could make his
voice answer her.

"Sure, sure I can."

He turned back to the car and grabbed the bag his
elbow had been resting on moments before. He looked
inside. Fresh doughnuts from Waite's Bakery in Bracebridge! Well, even if they were a bit squashed, they'd
still taste good. The back seat was full of stuff. It was
going to take him forever.

Then Sarah's voice startled him.

"I'll help," she said, letting go of her grip on Mum.
She headed back to the car.

Would wonders never cease! Taking her rowing and
berry-picking and teaching her to do a duck-dive were
paying off.

"About time you started earning your keep," he
growled.

She made no answer. Looking down at her, he saw
in her eyes his own uneasiness.

"Take the doughnuts and bread first," he told her,
handing them over. "And don't mash them, either."

"I won't," she said meekly and started off in the direction the others had taken.

He stared after her. She loved doughnuts more than anything except licorice, and yet she had not looked even faintly pleased. He couldn't stand it if even Sarah started acting strangely. Wishing she would snap out of it, he opened the trunk and took out the two big suitcases. Staggering under their weight, he lugged them into the cottage. He would have carried them all the way into his parents' bedroom, but the door was closed.

"Don't pretend you're not exhausted, Adrian," he could hear his mother's voice saying. "Jeremy and I will bring the things in. You rest until it's time for supper."

Sarah, standing near the closed door, stared from it to her brother, her eyes wide.

"Is Daddy going to take a nap?" she asked in a whisper.

Jeremy did not blame her for being confused. He could not remember Dad ever having a rest in the daytime. They both heard him answer, "I'm all right, Melly. Don't fuss over me." Then he added wearily, "But I will lie down all the same even though I barely said hello to Margery."

"She understands," Mum replied.

This wasn't the way Jeremy had thought it would be. It had been weeks since he had last seen his father. He had barely said hello to him, either. He stood still for a long moment. Then he beckoned to Sarah and made for the door. She followed without a word.

When they were a safe distance from the house, he turned to face her.

"He's been sick, you dope," he said, sounding impatient as if he knew exactly what he was talking about. "Everybody has to rest more after they've been sick."

"But I thought he was all better," Sarah objected.

"It takes time," he said vaguely, putting her off just

as Aunt Margery had done to him. ''Don't worry about it. Everything's going to be fine.''

Then he went trudging back to the car. There was lots more to bring in and he expected her to follow. He was taken aback when he went to hand her something and found she was not there.

He saw her flying toward Mum who had come out onto the top step. She was waiting with arms outstretched and, the next instant, Sarah was folded in a big hug. Jeremy, still clutching the shopping bag he had meant to hand over to his sister, took a couple of steps toward Mum himself. But he stopped in his tracks when he saw the two of them walking off toward the swing, hand in hand, not even noticing they were leaving him behind. Quickly, before they could see him, he wheeled around and hauled the last armful of things out of the trunk.

It was too much for him to carry all at once. He had to make two trips. Nobody noticed. Dad was still in the bedroom and Aunt Margery was setting the table out on the porch. Fetching in the last few things, Jeremy dumped them down on the couch, deliberately dropping them so that they would tumble over each other and send at least a couple of items slipping onto the floor. Let Mum pick up the pieces when she finished giving that little sucky baby Sarah a swing! Too bad if something was broken. Just too damn bad!

Swearing inside his head made him feel slightly better. Then, hearing Aunt Margery starting back into the living room, Jeremy took off. If they wanted him, they could come looking for him. He'd done his share.

Four

Jeremy was just about to let the screen door slam behind him when he remembered that his father might be asleep. He closed the door carefully and headed for the lake. One thing was certain, he wasn't going near the swing. Not that they'd notice him if he did!

Suddenly his attention was caught by something floating in the water close to the shore. Forgetting how mad he was at his family, he went running down to investigate.

It was three weather-beaten boards held together by a fourth plank nailed across them. It looked like part of an old dock. Jeremy got his sneakers wet as he hauled it ashore. What a neat raft he could make out of it, especially with Dad here to help him. Then he and Luke and Mark Moffat could go somewhere when they came up. They could pole it along and go. . . where?

Nowhere.

The answer came to him like a punch in the stomach. He had forgotten for those few seconds that the Moffats, his best friends since grade two, had moved to Vancouver while he had been up at the cottage. He had forgotten that Dad was sick, too sick to get out of the car himself, much less build a raft. He had even forgotten that they were a week into August and the summer would soon be over.

Jeremy dropped down onto the rock beside the boards he had just rescued and stared out over the lake.

Who was he going to hang around with this year? Without the Moffats, who'd he have for friends? Oh, he'd find somebody, but he wished he knew who. At least he'd be in grade six, one of the big kids.

"Jeremy," his mother's voice called.

"Coming!" he yelled, scrambling to his feet.

His grudge against her disappeared as he went racing back up the hill to the cottage. She was waiting for him just outside the door. When he arrived, out of breath, she grabbed him and hugged him hard. Then she looked down into his eyes and said, "I missed you, Jeremy Talbot."

"I missed you, too."

It was the exchange the two of them had used each day when he came home from nursery school. He was too old for it now, of course, and she had not said it in years. But right now it let both of them say what they were really feeling in a way that was safe and familiar.

"Supper," Aunt Margery called to them in a clear but low voice. "Come in quietly. I think Adrian has fallen asleep."

When Mum saw the meal Aunt Margery had prepared, she shook her head in wonder.

''Margery,'' she said, ''I hope you realize that you've spoiled the children for the suppers I throw together up here.''

Aunt Margery flushed a little but she looked pleased. Then Sarah piped up.

''I like your cooking way better than this, Mummy.'' Catching her mother's eye, she tried to explain and only made things worse. ''Aunt Margery always cooks city food. I like cottage food best.''

''Not another word until you finish every bite of those vegetables,'' Mum said firmly. ''I never heard such in-gratitude and I'm ashamed of you.''

Sarah was crushed. Jeremy sympathized with her even though he knew she had been rude and embarrassed Mum. Putting out his foot, he nudged his sister's ankle gently with his toe.

He agreed with her completely. Meals at the cottage had always been casual affairs, with everybody expected to take his or her turn not only at dishwashing but at planning and preparing the food as well. Sarah still needed some help, but he could now get a whole meal ready entirely on his own. He was especially good at concocting new varieties of pizza, and he was the best egg-scrambler in the family.

Things had been different this summer. Aunt Margery hadn't wanted them in the kitchen. She had never come right out and said so but they could tell. It was just as well, as she disapproved of mixes and frozen foods. Jeremy had a feeling he wouldn't be such a success if he had to make a pizza from scratch.

Sarah recovered quickly. After only two bites of mixed vegetables, she launched into a rambling, involved ac-count of every single solitary thing they had done during the five weeks Mum had been away from them. She was boring, and Jeremy was about to demand equal time when his aunt cut in smoothly, "If I might be permitted to get a word in edgewise, Sarah. . ."

Sarah sputtered to a stop. Aunt Margery looked at the food still on her niece's plate and raised her eyebrows. Then she murmured, "Did I hear something about you eating up your vegetables?"

That was mean, Jeremy thought. He had wanted to shut his sister up himself but he wouldn't have done it that way. Sarah glared, was about to retort, but then swallowed and held her peace as Mum's arm went around her. Aunt Margery pretended not to see that little hug and began to talk for what seemed like hours about her problems with the water filter, some argument she'd had with Mr. Tweedy at the trailer camp and other tedious grown-up things. Only once was there a pause long enough to allow Jeremy to jump in and begin to tell Mum about a snake he had seen eating a frog. Aunt Margery shuddered, Sarah gave a little shriek, and Mum said he could tell her later since it wasn't of general interest.

As if he had been interested in the dumb old water filter! How he wanted to get away from this mob of women, to go in to talk to his father. Dad wouldn't squeal and fuss like an idiot. Dad would be interested.

Jeremy stared at his plate and tried to gulp down the lump that had come into this throat.

Then he heard his aunt say, 'To be fair, Melly, I don't suppose the children find my troubles with the water filter to be of general interest. Jeremy has better manners than I do. Everybody ready for dessert?"

Jeremy helped her clear away the plates. Aunt Margery removed Sarah's with the vegetables still on it without comment. She was okay, really.

He was the first one finished with dessert since, in spite of what Aunt Margery had said, she and Mum got talking about more boring stuff. They dawdled over coffee, too. He had waited to see his mother for so long that he stuck around, hoping for a chance to talk with her. When no chance seemed to be coming, he asked to be excused. He was mad and he didn't try to hide it. Mum flashed him an understanding grin but she went on listening to Aunt Margery.

He sprawled on the couch where he could keep an eye on Dad's bedroom door and leafed through some old comics he knew almost by heart. But Dad had still not wakened when Mum summoned Jeremy to lend a hand with the dishes.

Then Aunt Margery came out to tell them Dad was awake.

"I'll take his plate in to him, Melly," she said.

As his aunt busied herself serving Dad's supper, Mum put down her dish towel and went to see if there was something he needed. Jeremy, his back turned to his aunt, was furious. Longing for a chance to talk with Dad, here he stood with his hands in the dishwasher, while Aunt Margery, who usually did the dishes, was free to go and sit with him. Trust her!

As he reached for the first of the pots, Jeremy heard her pause to speak to Mum on her way back. The two of them would probably stand there gabbing while he slaved all alone and his father's dinner got cold.

Feeling the urge to murder both of them, Jeremy banged

the pots together and sloshed some water onto the counter. Mum, arriving just in time to catch him at it, chuckled.

"Only four more things to wash and you'll be done," she consoled him. "Then what would you say to an evening dip?"

His anger evaporated instantly. They had not been in swimming after supper all summer. He hurried, and in no time the three of them were down at the water's edge. He shed all his troubles along with his towel, raced the length of the dock and leaped into the lake. They had a marvellous time. Sarah showed off her duck-dive and Mum was impressed not only with her but also with Jeremy for teaching her.

As they started climbing the hill to the cottage, Jeremy pushed ahead of the other two. They had been gone plenty long enough for Dad to have finished eating. Surely he and Aunt Margery had talked to each other long enough, too. Now it was his turn. When he arrived at the door, however, his aunt was on hand with her finger raised to hush their noise.

"Adrian did eat," she told Mum over Jeremy's head, "although not as much as I'd have liked him to. He said he was too tired. I made him lie right back down and when I peeked in a couple of minutes ago, he had dozed off again."

Jeremy was so disappointed that he came close to bursting into tears. In frustration, he snapped the end of his towel against Sarah's bare leg. He missed, but she screeched anyway. Mum paid no attention to the shriek.

"Jeremy, he'll be much more himself tomorrow and you'll have lots of time together then, I promise," she said. Then she changed the subject. "If you get into your pajamas, we can pop some corn and I'll read."

Jeremy's heart lifted. He liked it when she read to them. She always picked neat books and she made the stories come alive as she read them. But he didn't want to give up his bad mood too quickly. He looked at her without a hint of a smile.

"Did you bring something new?" he demanded.

His mother grinned.

"I brought *five*," she told him. "I'll get them all and you can choose."

He chose one called *The Great Gilly Hopkins*. Mum read for a long time, but when she finally closed the book, Adrian Talbot was still asleep.

Five

The moment he woke up the next morning, Jeremy heard the rain tapping on the roof. He smiled to himself. He liked rainy days at the cottage as long as there weren't too many in a row. It meant spending time indoors but the cottage was cosy with the murmur of rain on the roof and a bright fire blazing in the Franklin stove. He and Sarah could play Monopoly. Maybe Dad would be well enough to play with them. Surely he must have rested enough by now.

The knowledge that Aunt Margery was leaving right after breakfast added to Jeremy's pleasure. He knew he shouldn't be glad but he couldn't help it. She was an extra now that Mum and Dad had come. The four of them were a complete family by themselves.

When all of them but Dad were gathered at the breakfast table, Aunt Margery said, "I'm not going back to London just yet, Melly. I'm going over to visit Esther

Enright on Skeleton Lake. That way, I can come back on Thursday. Adrian reminded me that it's your birthday. I'll be back in lots of time to bake the cake.''

"And put the money in?'' Sarah said hopefully.

Everyone laughed.

"And put the money in,'' Aunt Margery agreed. ''I can stay then and help you get packed. It's a shame you can only be up here such a little while.''

"Such a little while?'' Jeremy and Sarah spoke together, dismay in their voices.

"Your father has to go into the hospital for some treatment,'' Mum explained, ''so we'll have to go back to town early this year. But not quite yet, so don't look so mournful. We still have a whole week.''

Then Aunt Margery went dashing through the rain to her car. They leaned out the door to wave goodbye. At last the four Talbots were alone.

Fifteen minutes later, while Mum was cleaning up the breakfast dishes, Dad woke and called her. Jeremy sprang up, eager to go. His mother smiled and nodded. When Dad saw him, he smiled, too.

"My, Melly, how you've shrunk!'' he said.

"She's busy in the kitchen,'' Jeremy explained with a grin.

"Never mind. You'll do. Would you hand me that bottle of pills on the dresser?''

Jeremy looked. It was the only bottle there. As he picked it up, he saw typed on the label, ONE OR TWO TABLETS EVERY FOUR HOURS AS REQUIRED FOR PAIN. He flushed as he put the bottle into his father's outstretched hand. He felt as though he had been snooping. If Dad noticed, he gave no sign. He held out an empty water glass to be filled.

As Jeremy ran the water from the special drinking-water tap, he said to his mother in a low voice, ''He's taking pills.''

Mum didn't look surprised.

''Tell him his blueberry muffins and bacon will be ready in five minutes,'' she said. ''I'll take them in to him if he isn't feeling strong enough to make it to the table.''

Jeremy delivered the message with the water. Dad made no reply until he had swallowed a pill. Though Jeremy had not tacked on what Mum had said about not being strong enough, Dad must have heard her.

''Tell her that, so far, I've never been too weak to make it to a blueberry muffin.'' But he did not get out of bed. He looked down at the glass he was still holding and added, ''Ask her to make it fifteen minutes, though. I'm still only half awake. Okay?''

Jeremy nodded, turned and bolted out of the room. His father, who had claimed for years that he didn't believe in taking medicine, any kind, was waiting for that pill to work. Mum must have understood, too. She took her time finishing up the rest of the dishes and tidying the kitchen before she started preparing Dad's breakfast.

Jeremy wandered back into the living room and sat down before the fire. Hugging his knees, he watched the flames leap and dance and listened to them crackle. Behind their snapping, he could hear the rain drumming on the roof and Sarah's voice as she chatted softly to her doll, Fiona. The tight knot of worry inside him loosened.

Then Dad came out and took his place at the table. Jeremy saw, without wanting to, that he moved differently now. Slowly, carefully, as if he were afraid he might break. The instant he was settled, Mum brought in some muffins and hot coffee.

"Your bacon will be ready in a minute," she told him, giving him a smile before she turned to go back to the kitchen.

Jeremy got up to join his father.

"Guess what," he started to say. "Yesterday I saw a Baltimore oriole. . ."

But Sarah got in one second ahead of him.

"Daddy," she said, "what's a fifty-fifty chance?"

Jeremy stopped in his tracks. Mum, who had gone for the bacon and was on her way back, almost bumped into him. Seeing his expression, she paused and followed his gaze to Sarah's face. But Dad was answering already.

"It means half-and-half, Sarah. Why?"

"Paul Denver said that his mother said you have a fifty-fifty chance. Chance at what?"

"Leave your father alone while he eats," Mum said quickly. "Adrian, there's no need to go into it right now."

Adrian Talbot looked across at her.

"They had better hear it from us, Melly, rather than from somebody else. You would think Margery would know that Joan Denver can't keep anything to herself."

He moved on his chair so that he faced Sarah.

"You know that I had an operation, don't you?" he asked. When Sarah nodded, he went on. "Well, sometimes when people have an operation, they're all better and sometimes. . ."

"They're half-and-half?" filled in Sarah doubtfully.

"Adrian, don't push yourself," Mum broke in again.

"It's okay, Melly."

Mum began staring hard at the fire. Jeremy didn't think

she was seeing it, really. Sarah, feeling the growing tension, began to chew the edge of her thumbnail. Jeremy gazed out through the big window at the grey lake, swept with rain. He tried to detach himself from the warm room and from his certain knowledge that his mother was fighting not to cry.

"It's time we talked about it," Dad said to the two of them. When neither replied, he said in a firm, strong voice, "Sarah, I have cancer."

Sarah took her thumb out of her mouth and stared at him.

"But you don't smoke."

Mum and Dad both laughed. Jeremy was not sure why. It had been his first thought, too. But Dad went on to make himself clear.

"There are other kinds of cancer besides lung cancer. I don't have lung cancer."

"What kind do you have?"

Jeremy was glad Sarah was asking all the questions. He could not have made words come through the tightness in his throat.

"It isn't easy to explain," Adrian Talbot said. "But I had an operation to see if they could remove it."

This time Sarah did not pop in a question when he paused.

"I waited too long," her father said. "But I'm going to have treatment, a different kind of treatment. I have to go to Hamilton every two weeks. They hope that will help. Now, how about letting me get on with my breakfast?"

He picked up his muffin and Sarah, satisfied, went back to playing with Fiona. But Jeremy, his knees feeling wobbly all at once, sank back down in front of the fire and returned to staring at the flames.

Cancer! But cancer killed people!

As though she could read his thoughts, Mum said, "Several people we know have had cancer."

Jeremy looked at her, hope rising in him.

"Margery had skin cancer," she went on. "Just a little patch on her face. That's why she wears a hat whenever she's out in the sun for any length of time. They removed it without any trouble. And Mr. Barr, Jeremy, right next door to us, did have lung cancer. He had a lobe of his lung taken out ten years ago and he's been fine ever since. Anyway, we mustn't let the word 'cancer' scare us too badly. Now, anybody for a game of Monopoly?"

Jeremy's mouth dropped open. Sarah sprang to her feet with a squeak of delight. Yet deep inside Jeremy was the knowledge that Mum was only going to play to distract them, to keep them from dwelling on what she and Dad had been saying. Still it was wonderful to have his mother play. She must be glad to be back with them! She loathed Monopoly. The only trouble was that whenever she played, she won.

"I get to be banker," he said.

"No, I get to be banker," Adrian Talbot said, "because I'm the oldest."

It was a marvellous morning. When Mum declared that she had obviously won and refused to play any longer because it would be too cruel bankrupting the rest of them, Jeremy felt the ordinary world settling comfortably into place around him. It was like getting back into your jeans after church, or like snuggling down with your very own pillow after sleeping at another boy's house where all the pillows were bouncy instead of soft. It was a wonderful feeling, he thought. They had all come home where they belonged.

Six

When they were eating lunch, Jeremy looked at his father. Dad was sitting by the window and gazing far away over the lake. He seemed so remote that he was almost not there with them. His sandwich lay untasted on his plate.

Jeremy reached out for the jar of mustard pickles.

"Dad," he said, touching his father's limp hand with the side of the jar and hearing his voice sounding out too loudly, "would you care for some pickle?"

"Get *him!*" Sarah said.

"I knew I could do it and I have," Mum cried. Her voice also rang out unnaturally.

Dad's attention was caught.

"Do what?" he asked listlessly.

"I have raised a son who is a gentleman."

"Yuck," commented Sarah.

''Well, congratulations to you and your gentlemanly son,'' Jeremy's father said.

It sounded ordinary enough. Now Dad began to eat, too. But he didn't seem very hungry. He said nothing more and he did not take any of the pickle. Jeremy glanced at Mum. She was watching Dad. She looked so anxious that Jeremy ate his apple for dessert without tasting it.

After lunch, Mum started a giant jigsaw puzzle but Dad, instead of joining in, went back to bed. Mum tried to encourage them to get the edge pieces, but their father was the best at puzzles. When Jeremy and Sarah began to bicker in their usual fashion, Mum kept telling them to hush. It was not an easy thing to do in a cottage with walls so thin that they let through every sound. Finally Mum lost her temper and turned the pair of them right out of the house.

Jeremy liked playing in the rain, but not when it wasn't his own idea. Bored, he caught a particularly large bullfrog and chased Sarah with it. She didn't mind frogs as a rule but this one was enormous and Jeremy was in such a mean mood that she grew panicky and fled, screaming, to Mum.

She had her revenge. Jeremy was dispatched on a lonely walk to the trailer park to get a jar of instant coffee and some skim milk, neither of which were of any interest to him. He clumped along the road, hating his sister. It took him nearly half an hour to get to the store. By the time he got there, he hated his parents, too.

Late in the afternoon, Dad got up again, but he buried himself in a book. Mum and Sarah were together in the kitchen, beginning to get supper organized. Jeremy stood in the middle of the living room and wondered what he should do. He hoped his father would notice him standing there and put down his book, but he didn't.

That evening, when Sarah was asleep and Jeremy was in bed reading, Mum called in, "Jeremy, your father and I are going out for a short walk. Just shout out the door if you want us. We won't be far."

That was the last straw. All day long, it seemed to Jeremy, Dad had been sitting or lying around as though he was too sick to do anything active like going for a walk. So Jeremy had not asked even once. And now he was to be left minding Sarah while they went out!

"Did you hear me, Jeremy?" Mum came to his door to check.

"Yeah, I heard."

He could hear the grouchy note in his own voice but Mum didn't seem to notice. She disappeared and a moment later he could hear the screen door open and close behind them. Mum murmured something and Dad laughed.

Were they laughing at him?

Then, in a matter of minutes, the screen door opened again and Mum was there beside him. She had some raindrops caught in her hair and her face was all rosy.

"Jeremy, go out to your father right now. Just put on your thongs. Don't stop for a jacket even. Oh, wait. Take this."

She thrust a flashlight into his hand. He had scrambled out of bed but he felt bewildered. Was it some kind of a joke?

"He's at the far end of the parking space," she hurried on, pushing him ahead of her as she talked. "Don't put the light on till he tells you. Be careful not to make a racket. *Go!*"

He did not understand any of it but he was suddenly

full to bursting with joy. Dad did want him. He wanted
him right this minute.

"Over here, Jeremy," he heard his father whisper.

It was really dark already. It would have been spooky if
it weren't for Dad waiting for him, watching him come.

"Here I am," Dad's voice murmured as he reached
out and pulled Jeremy to stand close beside him. A long
drip of cold water went down Jeremy's warm back. He
flinched but made no sound.

"Let me have the flashlight," his father said.

Jeremy passed it over. Dad turned it on to the low
beam and, shielding half of the light with his hand, he
shone it up into the tree above them.

"Look," he whispered. "Look hard. There were two
of them but one went swooping off while your mother
was getting you. Can you see it?"

Jeremy knew it must be a bird. He and his father were
always on the lookout for birds. Today on the way to
the store he had seen a goldfinch, a brown thrasher and
two cedar waxwings. But up there, there was nothing.
Nothing but a . . . well, it looked like a small bundle of
something roundish. It reminded him of Pooh Bear sitting on the branch waiting to be rescued by . . .

Then, without warning, he saw two eyes open, two
huge golden eyes. He had never in his life seen such
round eyes. Dad shone the light full up at the owl then,
but Jeremy never did see more than those magical orbs
of black and gold, for the owl unfurled itself, became a
winged darkness and was gone. Just as Jeremy was beginning to breathe again, certain it was all over, he heard
the bird give a call, a funny, irritated, not unfriendly
"Hoot."

"Oh, Dad," he whispered, "it really hooted. I thought it was like pigs saying 'Oink' or dogs saying 'Bow-wow' but it wasn't. It said, 'Hoot.' I thought . . ."

"I know," his father said and drew his son close against him, heedless of the waterfall the owl had shaken down on them when it took flight.

"It had owl eyes. Did you see the eyes?"

"Yes. I've never seen an owl's eyes before, not like that. I've seen owls in zoos, of course, and in pictures and sometimes, in winter, I've seen them perched up in bare trees. But this one". . .

"This one," Jeremy broke in, too excited to let Dad finish, "looked right at me and it hooted. Just the way they're supposed to."

The two of them were repeating themselves but it didn't matter. It was as if they had been turned into one person by what they had shared. Jeremy did not even know he was shivering.

Then a bright light came bobbing toward them. They were silent, watching Melly Talbot come.

"They're gone, aren't they?" she asked when she was near enough. "I could hear you talking so I knew they must be. Did you see them, Jeremy?"

"One left before he got out here," Dad answered. "But the other one looked right down at us and we saw its eyes clearly. Then it unbundled itself and swooped clumsily away. Astonishing, wasn't it, Jeremy?"

But Mum broke in before Jeremy could reply.

"Adrian, you are sopping wet and Jeremy is still in his pajamas! I must be losing my grip letting the two of you stand out here and freeze. Come on in where it's warm."

They went obediently after her, but not until they had

paused for a wordless moment, Jeremy's hand held tightly in his father's, to look up into the sky where somewhere their owl must be. When they were entering the cottage, Dad laughed all at once.

"What's a bit of water matter?" he said. "Get this, Jeremy. We don't give a hoot!"

Seven

Things got steadily better after that. The next morning Dad went outside and lay in the hammock. He brought the bird book and the binoculars, and he and Jeremy spent a happy hour bird-watching. Later on he went for a stroll with Sarah, holding the bowl for her while she picked berries. Soon he had a bit of sunburn and was no longer the chalky white he had been when he had arrived. Each day that passed, he seemed to get a bit stronger and be more his old self.

Jeremy began to relax. If Dad was still taking those pills, he had not caught him at it. And Sarah had stopped asking awkward questions.

The afternoon before Aunt Margery was due back, Jeremy and Dad went for a walk, just the two of them. They were a short distance from home when Adrian Talbot said, "Let's sit down for a minute. There's something I want to talk over with you."

Jeremy perched himself cross-legged on a jutting ledge of granite. Had he done something to make Dad mad at him? He couldn't think of anything that would require a lecture in private. His father, catching his worried expression, gave him a reassuring grin.

"Relax. Your sins have not found you out. It's something quite different I want to discuss with you."

Jeremy settled himself more comfortably and waited, his curiosity aroused. But Dad seemed lost in thought all at once. Seconds ticked by. Then, just as Jeremy felt ready to burst, his father struck him dumb with astonishment by saying, "Do you know Tess Medford?"

"Tess Medford!" Jeremy echoed stupidly after a long pause. "You mean the Tess Medford at school?"

He knew the answer before Dad nodded. There couldn't be more than one Tess Medford. But why. . .?

"Yes, the Tess Medford at school," Dad said drily. "She was in my class last year, as I'm sure you remember."

Jeremy looked down at the rock on which they were sitting and began picking at lichen. He remembered her, all right. Tess was taller than any boy at school. She was taller than most of the teachers, even. But it wasn't just that. She was weird. Not only didn't she wear jeans, like everyone else; she wore big, baggy old-lady dresses that made her stick out like a sore thumb. And worst of all, she didn't seem to care. It was almost as if she was proud of being different.

"She's going to be in your room in September," his father went on. "I saw the class lists when I was in the office. . . She's had a rough time. I hoped to be able to help her but I won't be going back to work for awhile. . .

I suspect she's very lonely. I just thought that maybe, now that Luke and Mark are gone, you might try making friends with her. If you did, the others would soon follow.''

Jeremy was appalled. Him be friends with Tess Medford? Dad must be crazy. Not only was she a girl, but nobody in his right mind would choose Tess as a friend. Dad didn't need to worry about her. She could take care of herself.

"I don't think she wants friends," Jeremy mumbled, not looking at his father. "She doesn't know the rest of us are alive. I hardly know her, Dad, but I've heard some of the others talking about her. Right from the first day, she was . . . well. . .stuck up. The girls tried to be nice to her but she just snubbed them. I wouldn't know how to begin. . .''

Jeremy couldn't seem to stop explaining. Then his father cut in.

"Forget it," he said, his voice flat. "I shouldn't have suggested it. It was just that she seemed to be coming out of her shell a little last spring. . . . But it wasn't fair of me to ask you to befriend her. I'm rested now. Let's go on as far as the turn-off.''

He heaved himself up from the rock and set off down the road without waiting for Jeremy. The boy scrambled down from his perch and ran after him. Before he quite reached the man's side, however, he slowed so that he was walking along a step or two behind. He felt miserable. He could tell Dad was disappointed in him. But it wasn't his fault. Why didn't Dad understand? Finally, desperately, he gave a spurt, caught up and made another attempt to explain.

"It isn't that I don't want to help," he burst out. "But she really doesn't want friends. Honest. It's not just because she's a girl. . ."

"I already told you to forget I ever mentioned it," Adrian Talbot snapped. "I wouldn't have if I hadn't faced the fact that I won't be back."

Won't be back for awhile, Jeremy thought. That's what you said last time. Won't be back for awhile. He did not speak his thoughts aloud but his father must have guessed. Suddenly he was himself again.

"I'm sorry," he said. "I didn't mean to lose my temper. I can't seem to help it these days. I suppose it's because I can't get used to . . . to not being well. I do understand how you feel. I'd probably feel exactly the same in your place. It's always hard at your age to accept people who are different. . . . Let's start back. It's ridiculous but I feel worn out already."

When they reached home, Jeremy went straight into his room and flung himself down on his bed. He did his best to make his mind a blank but the conversation with Dad kept nagging at him. It was not Tess Medford he thought about, but his father saying, "I won't be back." What had he meant? He'd have to go back sometime, wouldn't he?

Eight

Then Aunt Margery came back. She arrived in the evening, two days before Mum's birthday. The following morning at breakfast, Dad told them that he and Mum were going into Bracebridge for the day. Sarah and Jeremy were all set to join the expedition until Mum informed them that most of the time would be spent at the laundromat and the supermarket. Sarah still thought she wanted to go, but Dad distracted her by asking, "What would you like me to bring you, Sarah? That is if I should happen to have time and energy and money enough to buy you a surprise."

"Do you mean a present?" Sarah stared at him wide-eyed, not believing her ears.

"Well, tomorrow's your mother's birthday," Dad said with a grin. "So I *have* to get her something. I might just pick up one for you while I'm at it."

"Adrian, don't bite off more than you can chew," Mum warned. "I'm not sure you should even go into town."

"I don't think he should," Aunt Margery put in.

Sarah, seeing her present disappearing before it had even been purchased, looked anxious. Jeremy, who knew that if she got a gift, he would, too, felt much the same. Other kids' parents were always bringing them home gifts when they went places but his father and mother mostly restricted present-giving to Christmas and birthdays.

Dad gave his sister an annoyed look. "I won't do more than I can," he said irritably. "You leave me to worry about my own health. I've had enough good advice lately to last me the rest of my life."

Jeremy saw Mum turn her face away all at once. He felt a cold fingertip of fear touch him. Then he forgot it as Dad spoke to Sarah.

"If you don't *want* a present, Sarah, just say so."

"I do want one. I do!" Sarah cried. "I want a new doll to be friends with Fiona and I want some clothes for them and I want a doctor kit and I want . . ."

"Whoa!" Dad said. "I believe I said *one* present. That's enough out of you. Let your brother have a turn."

"Oh, he'll just say he wants a dog like always."

"If you would be so kind, Miss Talbot, I would prefer to hear Jeremy's request from his own lips," Dad said. "Now, Jeremy, how about it?"

"I just want a dog like always," Jeremy said, laughing.

"Oh, Jeremy, have some sense," Aunt Margery said sharply. "What on earth would your mother want with a dog right now?"

Jeremy shot her a disgusted look. It wasn't a dog for Mum that he wanted; it was dog for himself. He'd take care of it. He'd feed it and brush it and walk it and teach it tricks. But even as he thought about it, he knew they wouldn't get him one. They could always come up with a good reason not to. Wait till you're older. Wait till Sarah grows up a little. Wait, wait, wait! The truth was that they just plain did not want a puppy themselves and they didn't understand how terribly he wanted one. But he didn't want to spoil things for Dad.

"I'd like a bird book, I guess," he improvised quickly, trying to sound enthusiastic. "I'd really like a new bird book."

He was surprised when his father's face brightened. After all, the Talbots already had three bird books. Surely Dad must know he couldn't really want another. It was too late to take it back, though. In a few minutes, Mum and Dad had gone.

They didn't come back until Aunt Margery, Jeremy and Sarah had finished their supper. It was not a happy homecoming. Dad looked every bit as sick as he had the week before. Mum had to help him out of the car again. Jeremy and Sarah were left to lug in the bags of clean laundry. By the time that was done, Dad was in bed and Mum and Aunt Margery were talking in lowered voices in the kitchen.

"Where's my present?" Sarah demanded.

"Don't you mention the word 'present' to me!" Mum turned on her. "If it hadn't been for those fool presents. . ."

"Melly, you come and put your feet up," Aunt Margery said. She sounded bossy to the children but Mum looked at her gratefully. Making no protest, she let herself be escorted to the couch and deposited there. Their aunt went on, "I'll bring you a cup of coffee first and then I'll get you both something hot to eat. You look tuckered out."

Jeremy shook his head warningly at his sister. "Wait," he told her, grabbing her and holding her back from following. "Don't make her mad, stupid, or neither of us will get anything. Anyway, they're probably saving them for the morning." Then he added quickly, before she could begin to fuss, "Let's get our stuff for Mum wrapped. I'll help you."

That helped pass the time. Jeremy had bought his mother a denim hat and Sarah a little birchbark canoe that said "Welcome to Muskoka" on it.

At breakfast the next morning, Mum opened their gifts. There was no sign of any other presents. Jeremy thought Sarah would burst. He felt he could not wait much longer himself. Mum laughed at the looks on their faces. She got up and went into the bedroom. When she came out again, she was carrying a pile of boxes.

Sarah's presents came first. She was delighted by the scarlet box kite that her father promised to help her put together later.

"You can have a turn holding the string right after me," she promised Jeremy importantly. She had never had a kite of her own before.

Dad handed Sarah another box.

"Two presents!" Sarah breathed.

It was Fiona's new friend, an Indian princess doll.

"Her clothes come off, too," Mum said, knowing what was wanted when it came to dolls.

Finally Dad looked at Jeremy quizzically and passed over a book-shaped parcel.

"I'm sorry, but they weren't selling dogs in Bracebridge yesterday," he said.

There was something Jeremy did not understand in his tone of voice. Jeremy waited a moment but, when his father said nothing more, he opened the package and took out a new book about birds.

"Thanks a lot," he said, flipping through the pages dutifully. "It looks great. Thanks."

He did his best to sound pleased but it was difficult.

"If you knew how many stores your father went to trying to buy you your own binoculars," Mum said, on the edge of anger, "you'd be more appreciative. I told him you yourself asked for a bird book but he wasn't satisfied until we'd been to practically every store in town."

Binoculars of his own! What a great idea! Jeremy's face lit up as she talked. He smiled at his father.

"Thanks for trying," he said.

But the book was not, after all, the reason for Dad's secret-keeping expression. Now he put his hand in his pocket and took out a small squarish box.

"The book is really for Margery," he said with a chuckle. "We have enough bird books, as you know. She's the one who can't tell a hummingbird from a penguin. Pass the book over to your aunt."

Aunt Margery laughed. Mum looked astonished. Dad was clearly pleased with himself. But he kept the mysterious small box in his hand and went on talking.

"I wish you could have that dog you want so much, Jeremy, but, if you really think about it, you'll see that right now is not the time for our family to take on the raising of a pup. Your mother is going to be busy being the chauffeur and hospital visitor as well as doing all the other things she does already. So I'm sorry but. . ."

Jeremy felt his face flushing under his father's serious

gaze. He started to say that it was all right but, before he could get the first words out, his aunt broke in.

"Don't worry about Jeremy. He's a sensible boy. I'm sure he understands how impossible a dog would be under the circumstances."

Jeremy twitched with irritation and stared at the floor. Dad, though, turned on her, his face reddening with sudden anger.

"Why should he understand? He's not quite twelve. I'm nearly fifty and I can't understand. The circumstances, as you call them, are beyond any of our understanding."

"Stop it, Adrian," Mum said in a sharp voice.

Aunt Margery's eyes had filled with tears and Jeremy, feeling horribly uncomfortable, saw that her hands were trembling. Mum did not let the bad moment go on, however.

"Take pity on Jeremy," she went on, smiling reassuringly at him. "He's been waiting to open that box for ages and I'm dying to know what's in it myself."

"I . . . I'm sorry," Dad muttered. He did not look at either Aunt Margery or at Jeremy. He handed over the box.

It was much heavier than Jeremy had expected it to be from its size. It had a string around it. He took time to undo the knot. He was hoping against hope that it was something he would really like. He could tell that his father was sure it was perfect, whatever it was. Jeremy put the string aside. He took the lid off. The thing inside was wrapped in tissue paper. Through the folds, Jeremy could feel that it was hard. It was shaped like an egg. Then Jeremy had the tissue paper off and his present was lying in his hand.

An owl! Their owl, his and Dad's. It fitted into his cupped palm as though it had been made hand-sized on purpose. Except for the eyes, it was made of polished stone, smooth and hard. The eyes looked straight at him. They were golden with big black pupils and, although they were made of glass, they seemed real. The bird had a small, downward-curving brownish beak. Except for the beak, the eyes and the rosy circles that ringed them, the rest of the owl was as white as snow.

"It's Ookpik!" Sarah cried out in delight.

It did look like the picture in *Alligator Pie* except that it was not furry or feathered but smooth. It also looked like Archimedes in *The Sword in the Stone* and like Owl in the Pooh books.

Like all the owls in all the books, Jeremy thought.

Yet, at the same time, it was none of them but especially and only his. His fingers closed around it protectively as Sarah reached for it.

"I like it," he said. "Thanks. Thanks a lot."

The ordinary words did not express what he was feeling but he knew Dad understood. It had all been said as their eyes met.

Then Mum reached out her hand as Sarah had done, only Jeremy did let her take it from him. She cradled it in her palm and smiled down at it.

"Oh, Adrian, it's perfect," she said softly. "I love it."

Laughing, Dad took it away from her and returned it to its owner.

"You can't have everything, Melly," he said, gently teasing. "This is for Jeremy."

"What are you going to name it?" Sarah wanted to know, tagging after him as he went into his room a few minutes later to put it on his chest of drawers.

Jeremy stood, studying his owl, considering owlish names. Then it came to him.

''Hoot,'' he said.

Nine

T he rest of Mum's birthday flew by. The cake had four layers and Jeremy got the quarter. The next thing he knew, he was putting on his pajamas.

"Jeremy," Mum called in to him, "I want you to have a bath and wash your hair tonight."

"No!" he groaned. "Please, no. I'm really clean! And I'm completely exhausted. I haven't got the strength. I'll do it tomorrow night."

"Exhausted, my foot!" Mum said, coming after him.

Jeremy dove into his bunk, pulled the covers up to his chin and began to snore lustily. Then, just as she reached for him, someone knocked at the cottage door. His mother let go of his hair and straightened up. Whack! The back of her head collided with the top bunk. Jeremy, who hit his head at least once every two or three days, winced in sympathy as she yelped. Then the two of them listened to Aunt Margery as she went to answer the door.

"Come on in," they heard her call out.

"Please, not Joan Denver!" Melly Talbot muttered.

"Why, Mr. Tweedy!" Aunt Margery exclaimed. "How nice of you to drop by."

Mum went to see what was happening, with Jeremy at her heels. Mr. Tweedy, the owner of the nearby trailer camp, stepped inside and smiled around at all of them. He was holding a cardboard carton in his arms but he made no move to put it down.

"Sorry to bother you folks," he burst out, his whole manner flustered and somehow guilty, "but I'm in a bit of a bind and I thought . . . it came to me . . . that you just maybe might be able to help me out, if you see what I mean."

They didn't see. He appeared to be stuck. They all smiled encouragingly at him and hoped for the best. Mr. Tweedy breathed heavily and blushed.

"Come in by the fire," Dad offered. "We were about to have some coffee. Won't you join us?"

He gestured toward the semi-circle of chairs drawn up in front of the Franklin stove.

"Yes, please do," Melly Talbot urged.

"Thank you," the man said. "Thank you muchly."

But he stayed rooted by the door. Sarah, who had left her bed at the same time as Jeremy, came to everyone's rescue.

"What's in that box?" she asked straight out.

Mr. Tweedy looked relieved.

"Kittens," he said.

Before they could do more than gasp, he had gone down on one knee, placed the box on the floor and opened it. The five Talbots leaned forward as though someone had pushed a button that controlled them all. Then they each made a crooning sound which changed to a chuckle as the smaller of the two kittens immediately took a run at the side of the carton and did its level best to scramble out. The other kitten sat up, yawned, licked its whiskers and practically smiled up at them. It was charming and it knew it.

"Purrupp," it remarked.

Sarah had it up in her arms the next instant and the kitten snuggled its head under her chin and hummed loudly.

"Be gentle, Sarah," Mum cautioned.

At the same moment, the smaller kitten backed up, took a second running leap and startled itself as much as anyone when it toppled over the side of the box to land squarely on Jeremy's bare feet. Sarah promptly shifted the kitten she was holding, freed one hand and reached for it also. Jeremy came to its rescue in the nick of time. Sarah eyed with envy the one he now held.

"I'll swap mine for yours," she offered.

"Neither of them is yours or Jeremy's," Mum said, laying a firm hand on the back of her daughter's neck. "And what may I ask are you doing out here, anyway, Sarah Jean? You're supposed to be sound asleep."

Sarah shot her an indignant glance. How could she be expected to remain in bed when there were kittens in the very next room?

"Are they Siamese?" Aunt Margery asked.

"The mother is a Siamese. Who knows what the father is? As of this morning, they don't have a mother or a father," Mr. Tweedy said. He had been squatting down by the box. Now he straightened up and went on to explain.

The Frasers, a couple from out west, had come to the

trailer park early in June. Mr. Fraser had wanted to spend
the summer fishing and Mrs. Fraser had brought her
purebred Siamese cat which she was entering in the
C.N.E. cat show. What she did not know, but discovered
soon after they arrived, was that her precious cat was
pregnant.

"I'm telling you, the fur flew that day!" Mr. Tweedy
said. "Her hubby had let the cat out one night when his
wife was away. Said he couldn't stand the yowling. The
wife meant to start a cattery as a business. Anyway,
Shangrila had her litter at our park on Canada Day.
Only these two kittens. When I got up this morning, the
Frasers were gone, taking Shangrila along, but leaving
these two behind in this box. One of the women at the
camp is willing to take one. She likes the one the little
girl is holding but she'll take either. Now it's up to me to
find a home for the other one. They're both female, both
housetrained. I just sort of hoped that you people . . ."

Jeremy was not really listening. The tiny cat he held
was so different, so special. She was blue, to begin with.
A silvery blue. Her face, tail and legs were darker. A
charcoal blue, perhaps. It was hard to find the right words
to describe her. She was lively and curious, poking her
face up against his one second and trying to reach his
nose and pat at it the next. She was purring, but not with
an ordinary humming sound. It was rougher, a little
hoarse, something like the noise a kettle makes when it
is boiling furiously.

Jeremy moved her back a little from himself so that he
could see her face. It was small and pointed. She had
bright blue, wide-awake eyes. She trembled a little at
being held out over space but she did not cry or panic.

She was brave, although he could feel her heart thudding against his hands.

"How could anybody be so heartless?" Mum said.

"I don't know," Mr. Tweedy shook his head. "I'd keep one myself. They're cunning little creatures. But my wife has heart spasms if a cat comes near her. You're sure you don't want one?"

He was looking at Aunt Margery.

"I may be an old maid but I haven't yet taken to keeping a cat," she said, her voice crisp. "I'm afraid you're out of luck, Mr. Tweedy. My brother's family have all the animal life they need with two children and I'm definitely not interested. I do appreciate your problem, though. Have you tried the Denvers? I don't know . . ."

Then Adrian Talbot's voice cut through her words neatly, deliberately.

"What are you going to call your cat, Jeremy?"

Jeremy's eyes widened in disbelief. He stared across at his father. Dad was gazing back at him, his face deadpan, his eyes understanding. He meant it.

Jeremy did his best to keep his own face free of expression. He tried to answer as coolly as his father had put the question. Yet the words would not come until he had cleared his throat. Then, holding the kitten up in such a way that the joy which shone from his eyes was hidden by her head, he replied as matter-of-factly as he could manage.

"Her name is Blue."

Ten

"Adrian, have some sense," Aunt Margery snapped, her face shocked and angry. "Think of Melly. One thing she does not need right now is a cat."

Jeremy waited. Dad wouldn't back down, would he? But Aunt Margery had not finished.

"Men!" she stormed on, almost spitting out the word. "They never think of the work involved. A cat! At a time like this! Surely you can see for yourself that it's out of the question."

While she fumed, Jeremy watched his mother's face. At first she had simply looked flabbergasted. He didn't blame her. But the next minute he saw her smile. He relaxed.

"But, Margery, the very first time I set eyes on Melly, she had a cat on her lap," Dad was saying with a laugh. "As I remember it, *every* time I saw her in those days, that selfsame feline was draped over her shoulder or snuggled in her arms or weaving around her feet. I even brought it catnip, to get on her good side.''

As his father was speaking these words, Mr. Tweedy nipped across to where Sarah stood, scooped the other kitten out of her clutching hands, deposited it back in the carton and fled.

''Thanks a heap, folks,'' they heard him call back. Then his truck roared off up the lane.

''That was a neat getaway,'' Aunt Margery snorted.

Jeremy paid no attention to her. He was still watching his mother. He could tell by the look on her face that now she, too, was remembering long ago times.

''Her name was Lady Jane,'' Mum said in a soft, dreamy voice. ''Lady Jane Grey, really, because she was grey with a white shirt-front and white paws. My father gave her to me on my seventh birthday. All my other birthdays blur together in my mind except that one. It was a perfect day and the crowning surprise was when Father presented me with Lady Jane.''

Jeremy did not have to wonder any longer. Aunt Margery could say what she liked but Blue was his. He took her into his room. Both he and his mother had forgotten he was supposed to be having a bath and washing his hair. The kitten cuddled close to him.

When he tried to settle her down for the night, though, she began to cry. She had never been separated from her sister before. She prowled about, searching for something familiar. Then Mum got a box, put a clock in the corner of it, a hot water bottle on top of the clock and a sweater Sarah had outgrown on top of that. Blue sniffed at the arrangement and gave Mum a scornful glance that plainly said she was not fooled for a minute. Nevertheless, a few minutes later, she snuggled down and fell asleep, her nose tucked under her tail.

The next morning, while Mum and Aunt Margery were cleaning out the fridge and gathering up the dirty laundry, Sarah went over to where her father was sitting and leaned against him confidingly.

"Daddy," she said in a soft, coaxing voice, "Blue's really half mine, isn't she?"

Jeremy, on his way to carry some stuff out to the car, jerked around and waited, breath held. It would not have surprised him if Dad had said, "Yes." They often had to share important things. The pup tent belonged to both of them and so did the toboggan. But he couldn't share Blue. He couldn't. Dad put his arm around Sarah and held her in a gentle hug, but he said the kitten was all Jeremy's. He reminded her of her kite and her new doll.

"They aren't as good as a cat," she wailed.

She was right about that. Jeremy even felt sorry for her. Not sorry enough to offer to share Blue, though.

It felt strange leaving the cottage when August was not quite half over. Aunt Margery went first in her own car. Mum managed to wedge Blue's box so that it sat firmly on the hump on the floor between Sarah and Jeremy. She put a towel over the box so that it would be dark inside. Blue pleased everybody but Sarah and Jeremy by curling up contentedly and sleeping most of the way home.

Although it had been hard to leave the cottage, it was good to be home. Jeremy had not missed TV while he was in Muskoka. Still it was great to watch it again, even though he had seen most of the shows before. He liked being back in his own room, too, among his books and models. The most fun, though, was watching Blue explore the house. She crept around chair legs, her ears pointing sharply forward, her tail sticking up like an exclamation mark. She pounced on bits of fluff and chased wholly imaginary mice.

"What would she do if she met a real mouse?" Sarah wondered.

"Die of shock, I expect," said her father.

One of the best things about Blue, Jeremy thought, was the way she made Dad laugh. He invented games for her, rolling paper or tinfoil into balls and throwing them for her to scamper after, or drawing a string across the floor and watching her crouch down and then spring on it and wrestle it into submission. When she tired, he would take her up on his lap. There she would wrap herself up into an amazingly small ball and go fast asleep.

"She thinks she's Daddy's cat," Sarah said, stealing a sideways look at her brother.

Jeremy didn't mind. He felt deeply peaceful whenever he saw them — the tall, thin, tired man and the tiny cat resting together.

For the first few days, Sarah tried to win her over so that no matter what Dad said to the contrary, she would be a shared cat. Blue, however, would have no part of this. When Sarah reached for her, she would melt away, easily keeping just out of reach. But when Jeremy sat cross-legged on the floor she would come without being called and clamber up on his lap. She didn't do it always, not so that he could count on it, but often enough to make it clear that she believed he belonged to her whether she belonged to him or not. Having her to play with helped to ease the loneliness he felt now that Mark and Luke were gone.

You couldn't play with a cat all the time, though. He tried doing things with some of the other kids who lived on their street, but they were older than he was or closer to Sarah's age. Either way, it wasn't much fun. He ended up spending a lot of time reading and watching television.

Early one evening, after they had been home a little more than a week, Mum told him to go outside and get some fresh air.

"You've been hanging around this house all day," she said. "I approve of reading. I'm not against television. But I don't want you turning into a dormouse."

"What exactly *is* a dormouse?" Jeremy asked.

Mum laughed.

"I haven't any idea. All I know is, they keep falling asleep. Out you go and no more stalling."

He went to the park. He joined a bunch of people watching a baseball game. He didn't know any of the players and they weren't all that good, but it was something to do. He pulled a long spear of grass and stood there chewing on the end of it. He hoped things would get more interesting, but they didn't. Bored, he turned away and headed for home. He must have been out for twenty minutes. That would have to do.

He rounded the corner to go down his own block and saw Tess Medford coming toward him. She looked just as weird as he had remembered, with her too-long skirt flapping around her knees and her hair skinned back into a dumb-looking braid. At once, he remembered talking with Dad about her. Funny that he'd completely forgotten about it until now. He knew, really, that he had forgotten deliberately. He wished he could avoid meeting her but it was too late. Well, he'd just say "Hi" and keep moving. If he knew Tess Medford, she wouldn't even look at him. He'd told Dad the truth when he had said she didn't want friends.

He quickened his pace. She was getting close to him now. Maybe he wouldn't say anything. He didn't really know her, not to speak to. Probably she wouldn't even recognize him. Automatically he moved to one side of the sidewalk to let her pass.

Instead of going by, however, she stepped in front of him and barred his way.

"Is it true that Mr. Talbot is . . . is sick?" she asked abruptly.

Startled, Jeremy stood and stared at her without replying. She flushed, but she stood her ground and went on doggedly.

"I guess I shouldn't be asking you but I really want to know and I don't know how else to find out."

"Yeah," he found himself saying. "He is sick. He's got cancer."

He was surprised at himself for telling her that much and even more surprised by the relief it gave him to talk about it. Now that he had begun, it was hard to stop.

"It isn't lung cancer." The words kept coming. "He's tired all the time and he's a lot thinner. He's going to go to the hospital for some treatment."

"He's not . . . he'll get better though, won't he?" Tess blurted.

Jeremy stepped back. He hated her suddenly. She had asked the one question he had not dared ask even in his innermost thoughts.

"Don't be so dumb," he cried angrily. "He's getting better right now."

Then he dodged past her and ran. He ran right by his house. He ran until he was gasping for breath and he had a stitch in his side. Then he turned around and went home.

Unable to sleep that night, Jeremy lay and thought about Tess. What a nosy, stupid girl. Who did she think she was? He didn't care if she really was worried about his father. He remembered Dad saying once, ''Tess Medford is a pleasure to teach. She actually thinks! It's a refreshing change.''

Well, Tess wasn't the only kid his age who had brains. If he were in his father's class, would Dad say he was a pleasure to teach?

Jeremy turned over. Why hadn't stupid old Tess minded her own business? His father was no concern of hers!

Maybe his mother guessed he was feeling miserable. She often seemed to sense these things. Now she stuck her head in his bedroom door.

''Jeremy,'' she said, ''what happened when the canary flew into the blender?''

He propped himself up on one elbow, relief flooding through him.

''I don't know. What?''

''Shredded tweet,'' said Melly Talbot.

Jeremy groaned loudly and fell back onto his pillow. In three minutes flat, he was asleep.

Eleven

The night before school opened, Jeremy and Blue were alone in the kitchen, she watching intently while he loaded the dishwasher. Usually one of his parents would be on hand to supervise, but Dad had been in bed all day and, just as the rest of them had finished their supper, Dr. Ricker had arrived to pay a house call on his way home from his office. Mum had gone with him to the bedroom and Sarah was in watching television.

When Jeremy was nearly through, his mother saw the doctor out. They stood talking in low voices at the front door for what seemed a long time. Then she helped Sarah start undressing for bed. Hearing her leaving his sister's room, Jeremy paused, hoping she would come to the kitchen, but instead she returned to Dad. The boy sighed, put the soap into the dishwasher, closed the door and twisted the knob. Now he only had the big frying pan left to do. He scrubbed at it furiously. Then he was finished.

"Hey, Bluecat, I'm done with hard labour," he announced.

Blue stood up, stretched and then jumped into a low drawer he had left open. She proceeded to inspect the clean dishtowels in it with intense interest, the tip of her tail twitching ever so slightly to aid her concentration. Jeremy hurriedly lifted her out with a still-wet hand. She squirmed free, dropped to the floor and glared up at him, both her fur and her temper ruffled.

"I know you have clean feet," he apologized, "but Mum wouldn't approve. You don't want to get me in trouble, do you?"

Blue busied herself washing the base of her tail. She was not speaking to him.

Sarah, dressed in her nightgown, came to the kitchen door. The little cat appeared not to know she existed.

"I thought having a cat would be different," Sarah said. "Krista's cat sits on her lap and purrs and lets her put doll-clothes on it. When she says its name, it always looks up and sometimes it comes running."

"Blue's not a common, everyday sort of cat," Jeremy said defensively. "She doesn't just purr. Even Mum says she talks."

"Mum shut the piano this afternoon so she wouldn't play on the keys anymore," Sarah told him, smiling. "Blue yelled as if she was really mad and Mum said, 'Blue, don't you swear at me!' "

Jeremy laughed but Sarah's smile vanished as quickly as it had come.

"Mum says we can't come home for lunch anymore."

Jeremy forgot about Blue. He stared at his sister. They always came home at noon. She must have gotten it confused somehow.

"You always wanted to take your lunch," he said, filling in the silence while he thought.

"I know," she said, her voice forlorn, "but I could come home if I wanted to. Now we can't come home even if we want to."

"You probably got it mixed up." He put away the frying pan and shut the cupboard door with a small satisfying bang. "I'll go check. I think Blue wants to play hide-and-seek. Watch this."

He grabbed a large paper bag out of the broom closet and punched a couple of holes in it. Then he set it down on the floor, its open end toward the kitten. Blue flattened herself out and crept slowly toward the sack, as though she knew full well it hid a mortal enemy. Her tail bushed out like a bottle brush. Sarah laughed aloud. Suddenly Blue leaped into the bag and started batting at it from the inside.

"She's a lot funnier than Krista's cat," Sarah said.

"When she pokes her head out through one of those holes, you tell her how smart she is," Jeremy instructed. "I'll be back in a minute."

He left, pleased with the way he had kept his sister from tagging after him. Mum would not talk to him in the same way with Sarah standing by. When he reached his parents' room, however, the door was closed.

He hesitated. He could hear them talking inside. He knocked.

"Come in," Mum called.

At first he thought that Dad was asleep. Then he real-

ized that he couldn't be. Hadn't he just heard them
talking? But Dad looked as if he were unaware of either
of them.

"What is it, Jeremy?" Mum asked quietly.

She wasn't angry. But she did not sound welcoming.
He must have butted in at a bad moment.

"Sarah thinks she can't come home for lunch even if
she wants to," he explained. "I told her I'd come and
find out what you really said. I knew she must have it
wrong."

"No, she's right," his mother said, her eyes not on
him but on his father. "I was coming out to talk to you
about it in a minute. Dr. Ricker thinks your father should
go into the hospital for awhile. That means the hospital
in Hamilton. I'll be driving over there every day and I
won't be home to get lunch at noon. I took it for granted
that Sarah would be delighted. She begged to take her
lunch last year like that friend of hers."

"Yeah. I remember. Mercy Phillpot."

Mum laughed.

"How could I have forgotten that child's name even
for a moment? Well, I'll go and tuck Sarah in and reas-
sure her. I don't think she wants to come home that
much. She just likes knowing that I'm here." She smiled
at him, glanced from him to his father, and then slipped
out, leaving them alone together.

"Sarah will be happy about the idea once she gets
used to it," Jeremy said, feeling a need to break the
silence. "She'll be okay."

"How about Jeremy?" Dad looked straight at his son
all at once. "Will he be okay?"

"Sure. I can . . . I can do lots of things at school. Like
use the library. Luke and Mark . . . "

He stopped. Luke and Mark would not be there. And last year the library had been closed at noon. They weren't allowed to eat in the library, anyway. He glanced uneasily at his father. But he seemed to have drifted back to sleep.

Would it be all right to leave now? How long was Dad going to be away?

"How long . . . ?" he started to ask, speaking softly so as not to disturb Dad if he really had fallen asleep.

The man on the bed sighed a long sigh. He opened his eyes but he didn't say anything. Jeremy backed away from him a little. Then his father's voice reached out to him.

"I don't know how long, Jeremy. Nobody knows. Even the doctor doesn't know."

Silence swallowed the thin, tired voice again and Jeremy was out the door, running for his own room. Once there, he stood still panting as if he had come a long way and blinking hard as though he were on the verge of crying, even though his eyes were dry.

"It's not fair," he said in a low choked voice. "It's not fair."

He wished there was something he could do to help. He'd go with Dad if they would let him. He could stay by him and bring him pills and water. When he felt better, they could talk. He could say, "Remember when we saw the owl?" And Dad would smile.

But they wouldn't let him. He knew that much. If they only would, he really would go . . . even if it were awful, even if his father just lay with his eyes shut and his hands limp and empty.

Then, all at once, Jeremy knew what he could do.

A minute later he was picking up one of his father's hands and putting Hoot into it.

"I want you to take him with you tomorrow," he said, not turning to look at Mum as she came back into the room, concentrating his whole attention on this stranger who was his father. "He's neat to hold, you know. He's small but heavy and smooth."

"He's neat all right," Dad agreed, looking not at Hoot but at Jeremy. Then he held the tiny owl up and smiled exactly the smile Jeremy had been missing.

"Yeah," Jeremy said. His mother reached out and put her hand on the back of his head, the way she had often done ever since he was a little boy. It was a loving touch, an approving touch.

"Put him with my things, Melly," Dad said.

Mum moved away from Jeremy and took Hoot. Turning, she put him into her purse. Dad laughed.

"Don't you take him, lady!" he warned. "I can see you covet that owl. But he's Jeremy's. He's only loaned to me."

"Don't worry," Mum said lightly. Jeremy, looking at her, saw that her face was shadowed with sadness. "You already told me, remember? 'You can't have everything, Melly,' you said. 'The bird is Jeremy's.' I'll pack it with your other things in a minute."

"Good," Dad said. The tiredness was back.

Jeremy left. He found Blue waiting for him outside the door. She pretended she did not recognize him at first, just to keep him humble. He scooped her up into his arms and was comforted by the feel of her, warm and alive and purring with contentment. It helped him to push back in his mind the sick feeling he had had when he had seen the fear in his mother's eyes.

Twelve

"Hurry up, Sarah. You should be out of here in three minutes." Mum took the plate out from under Jeremy's toast and added it to the other dishes in the dishwasher. "Two more bites and you'll be done."

Sarah jammed both bites in at once and picked up her milk glass. Mum, instead of telling her not to take such big bites, tipped her chair, depositing her on her feet. Jeremy laughed.

"That's enough out of you," Mum grinned. "Don't forget your lunch and don't disturb your father. He needs all the sleep he can get. I'll be here when you get home, Sarah, and if by any chance I'm not, check in with Mrs. Barr."

They both nodded. They had been over this before.

"So long," Jeremy said.

Sarah turned on the step to kiss Mum goodbye but the door was closed behind them. Jeremy, catching the look on his sister's face, spoke quickly, pretending not to notice the tears springing up in her eyes.

"It's a dirty gyp that you get a fancy new lunch box while I have to put my stuff in an already-used paper bag."

It worked. She looked down at her brand-new scarlet lunch box.

"It's nicer than Alyson Kent's," she told him smugly. "Hers is tin and it doesn't have a thermos inside. It used to be her sister's, too. Mum bought mine just for me. She might get you one, too, if you asked her."

Jeremy didn't tell her that he wouldn't be caught dead carrying a shiny new red lunch box or one of any other colour. No kid his age would.

"Let's get going," he said.

"Are you going to walk with me?" Sarah asked, startled.

"Might as well," he said off-handedly. "My bike needs a new front tire."

As they neared the school building, he was glad of her company. He had known he would miss Mark and Luke, but he had not been prepared for the feeling that came of being singled out, stared at because of Dad. It had sometimes been rough having his father teaching in the schools he attended, but it was a thing he had grown used to. It had not dawned on him until now that everyone would know his father was sick. Well, not everybody. But the teachers would know already and the kids would have found out by noon. If people asked him questions, he would play dumb. That was the best way to handle it.

"Sarah," he instructed, "if they start talking to you about Dad being in the hospital, play it cool. Don't tell them things that are none of their business."

"What kind of things?"

"I don't know. How can I know what they'll ask you? But if they ask how Dad is, you don't have to tell them he had to go back into the hospital. Just say he's fine and act like you don't know anything."

"But why? Why, Jeremy?"

How could he explain why when he himself did not understand?

"What do you mean 'Why?' Don't be so dumb." He reached out and grabbed her by one arm. On the point of shaking her, he changed his mind and let her go with only the suggestion of a shove. "Forget it. Do me a favour and forget I said anything. Anybody who asks you anything should know better. Only an idiot . . ."

He made himself stop. She wasn't the one he was mad at. His voice grew more gentle.

"I didn't mean to yell at you," he said. "Tell them whatever you want, okay?"

She stared up at him, her face tense.

"I don't know what you mean," she said, her voice anxious.

"I don't mean anything. I was just goofing off. Now let's move. You don't want to be late on the first day."

She gave him an uncertain smile. They went down the walk to the school. Once inside the big doors, he turned with her in the direction of the primary classrooms. She shot an astonished look up at him.

"You don't have to take me. I know where Miss Goldberg's room is."

"What's your problem, kid?" he asked her, snarling like a bad guy on TV. "You ashamed to be seen with me?"

Flustered, sure he was teasing her but afraid she might

be wrong, Sarah wailed, "No . . . I just . . . I thought
. . . I mean . . ."

His lips twitched in spite of him. Why was he hanging
around with her, of all people? Why didn't he just ditch
her and go his own way? Never mind why. He put his
hand around her pointy elbow and propelled her in front
of him as though she were a vacuum cleaner. She squealed,
pretending to be terrified, as kids her age jumped out of
the way. Then they were at Miss Goldberg's door. Sarah's
friends, Krista, Mercy and Alyson, saw her arrive and
came flying to meet her. As he turned to go she called
after him, "I won't tell, Jeremy. I can keep a secret."

"What secret?" Krista demanded. The other two
pushed close to hear.

"Best of luck," Jeremy said with a grin and left.

As he ploughed through the throng of excited students,
he wished he had not said anything to her about keeping
Dad's illness to herself. She couldn't keep a secret, not
unless she had changed a lot since he had last been crazy
enough to tell her one. By now, Krista probably had it
out of her. Would she say that he had cancer? Probably.

"Jeremy Talbot, you're the very boy I've been looking
for!"

Rats! It was Mrs. Meigs, his grade five teacher. He had
not liked her last year and he could tell she had not
changed for the better over the summer.

"I was *so* sorry to hear about your poor dear father,"
she said, her voice sugar-coated.

Jeremy tried not to wince. She had fallen into step
beside him.

"Yeah, well, thanks," he muttered. What was he supposed to answer, anyway? He felt a pang of sympathy
for his sister, struggling to keep her secret.

"I'm so fond of your dear mother," Mrs. Meigs gushed on. Now she had hold of his shoulder. "I don't like to trouble her by phoning. She must be just frantic with worry . . ."

It wasn't a question but she somehow made it sound like one, leaving her words dangling in the air between them. Jeremy mumbled something unintelligible and tried simply smiling politely. He had a feeling he was not going to get away with it. He didn't.

"I know it isn't easy for you to talk about it, dear," Mrs. Meigs said, staring down at him. Her fingers dug into him. So did her eyes. "How *is* poor Mr. Talbot? I'm only asking because we're all so concerned about him."

"He's okay, Mrs. Meigs."

"I suppose you're too young to understand. Your mother naturally would hesitate to talk things over with you children. Is he still in the hospital?"

"Not still," Jeremy tried to hedge.

He should have known better. Mrs. Meigs was not stupid. Her eyes seemed to pull the thoughts right out of his mind. Her next words pounced.

"He's *back* in hospital, is that it?"

Jeremy nodded, feeling he had somehow betrayed Mum even though she had not mentioned not talking about his father's illness. Some nerve he had, telling Sarah to keep her mouth shut.

"When did he go back?"

"He's going this morning."

"He must be worse, then?"

"I don't know." It wasn't an out-and-out lie. Nobody had actually told him Dad was worse. Maybe he seemed worse but really was better.

"Oh, the poor dear man! Why, he can't be fifty yet!"

"Mrs. Meigs, did you know Miss Willis is looking for you?"

It was Tess Medford's voice. Tess herself loomed over them. Jeremy looked up at her, weak with gratitude.

"Oh, no. Where is she?" Mrs. Meigs fluttered.

"In her office, I think."

The teacher bustled off, not even pausing to say good-bye to Jeremy. He gave a long sigh of pure relief.

"Am I ever glad you found her!" he said, forgetting for a moment that he was angry at Tess.

Tess laughed.

"Miss Willis will get a surprise," she said.

"You mean she's not looking for her?"

"Not that I know of." The baffled look on his face made her laugh again.

"Don't worry about it," she said curtly. "Mrs. Meigs gives me a royal pain, that's all. She's out-and-out nosy but she makes it hard not to answer her questions. I know from experience. And besides . . . I wanted to do something to make up for . . . last week," Tess finally blurted.

Before Jeremy had time to answer, the tall girl had turned her back, spinning so that her long braid flew out just missing his nose. She strode ahead of him through the open doorway of the classroom. He ducked back to avoid the flying rope of hair. Then he followed her in. She was halfway down the outside aisle, heading for a desk at the back. Whatever he might have found to say, it was too late.

Thirteen

Jeremy liked his new teacher right from the first moment. In spite of his name, Mr. Darling did not gush or even talk all that much. He asked what they thought and he really listened to what they told him, as if their ideas mattered. He laughed, too, when somebody cracked a joke, if it were the least bit funny. Yet they could tell, without even needing to test it, that he would not put up with real goofing off. He wasn't one bit scared of the class going out of control the way Mrs. Meigs had been. Maybe this was partly because he was so big. He made even Tess look short.

Well, not short exactly, Jeremy thought. Maybe normal.

Some of the kids had been in Mrs. Meigs' room with him last year. The rest came from his father's class. Jeremy knew all of them at least by name. Mervyn Reuber sat in front of him, Katy McDonough across the aisle on his right and Nan Ackerman right behind him. They were all good kids as far he knew. But none of them could take the twins' place. The girls were out of the running just because they were girls and Merv was a brain who studied all the time. Besides, his house was in the opposite direction from the Talbots'.

Then there was Kim Chiong. Jeremy looked sideways at Kim and wondered whether the other boy remembered his first day in this school. Jeremy remembered it too well. He had found the new boy out in the hall by the water fountain and had taken it for granted that he was from Vietnam or Cambodia or some place like that. Doing his best to make him feel at home, Jeremy had asked, "Do you speak English?"

"All the time," Kim had said in a cool voice with no trace of an accent. "How about you?"

Jeremy still felt himself blushing a whole year later. Kim had lived right here in Canada all his life. He was as Canadian as Jeremy was.

Jeremy read a book while he ate his lunch. That gave him an excuse not to talk to anybody. No one interrupted him to ask about Dad.

When school was dismissed and the first day was over, Jeremy was about one-third of the way home when he saw Tess Medford go by him on the opposite side of the street. He watched her turn the corner and wondered idly what Mrs. Meigs had quizzed Tess about. She'd probably been completely bug-eyed to find out why Tess lived with her grandfather. Quite a few kids he knew had parents who had split up, but Tess was the only one who stayed the whole time with one grandparent.

It was at that moment that he heard Tess yelling.

"You creeps! How could you? I'll kill you, you miserable creeps!" she was screaming.

Jeremy stopped in his tracks. For an instant he stood frozen. Then he broke into a run. Five seconds later, he rounded the corner and saw Tess up ahead of him. She was fighting tooth and nail with three big boys.

As he stopped momentarily, trying to figure out what was going on, one of the boys pulled free and ran off, laughing loudly.

"Come on, you guys," he called back to his buddies. "That chick has gone out of her skull!"

The others paid no attention. Tess seemed to be doing her level best to bash their heads together. They were big, though, one of them as tall as she was and a lot heavier. As Jeremy watched, that one made a fist and clouted Tess as hard as he could on the side of her head. Tess staggered backward a few steps. Then she shook her head and charged forward again.

Jeremy, with a yell of outrage, went tearing to her defence. Afterwards he knew that if he had stopped to think it over even for a second, he would never have got involved. The smaller of the boys was considerably bigger than he was. But he didn't stop to think.

"Cut that out!" he bellowed as he dove at the smaller boy.

He got him around the knees in a low tackle. Although his weight was not great enough to send the boy flying, he did knock him off balance. Tess promptly moved in on the teetering bully, elbowing his friend aside just long enough, and slugged him square in the middle with all her strength. He doubled up and sat down hard, wheezing.

"Way to go," Jeremy yelled excitedly. The light of battle shone in his eyes. There was no time to gloat, however. The boy Tess's size was not about to be beaten by a mere

girl and he was mean. Jeremy was between him and
Tess. The boy drew back his hand and Jeremy was sent
sprawling, but not before he had bitten deeply into the
little finger of the boy's hand. The boy shook his hand in
the air and swore. Tess went for him then, head down,
butting into him and pummeling him with both fists at
the same time.

What scared them off in the end, Jeremy thought, was
this white-hot rage of Tess's. She had threatened to kill
them and now she seemed to be really trying to do it. At
last, cursing, the two boys joined their friend and loped
off down the street.

"You wait!" they bellowed back at them from somewhere in the next block. "We'll get you or die trying!"
Then all three were out of sight.

Jeremy laughed shakily and looked around at Tess.
What on earth was she doing? She had knelt down on
the ground and now was leaning hunched over something he could not see properly. And she was crying!
After she had come through the whole battle without
shedding a tear.

"What is it?" he asked.

She did not reply. Instead she was intent on untying a
piece of rope that had been used to close up the mouth of
a burlap sack. What was she up to? Why . . . ?

Then Jeremy saw something move inside the sack and
he began to understand.

Tess, still not giving him so much as a glance, finally
got the knot undone. She eased the dirty old bag open.
A calico cat looked out at them, growling and spitting
furiously.

"They were playing catch with her," Tess said, her

voice choked and raw. ''I heard her crying. I couldn't believe it. How could they?''

As Tess stopped to draw in a sobbing breath, the cat made a dash for freedom. It streaked past them, tore in behind one of the nearby houses and was gone. It was a miracle it wasn't hurt.

Thinking of Blue, Jeremy felt an anger as fierce as Tess's.

Tess got to her feet and began dusting off her skirt. She glanced at Jeremy and then looked away again, rubbing the tears off her cheeks with a quick motion that left her face streaked with dirt.

''Thanks for pitching in,'' she said gruffly. ''You're a pretty good fighter.''

Thinking back, Jeremy found himself grinning. They had sent those bums packing, that was for sure. And he had done his part. The biggest boy must have Jeremy's teethmarks on his finger. He felt pleased with himself and Tess. After all, it had been three against two. So what if one of them had been on the far side of the street. He could have come running back at any minute. If he had, they'd have settled him, too.

''You're not half bad yourself,'' he said.

Tess made no further comment. Instead she leaned down and picked up a button from the sidewalk. When she straightened up, both of them saw that the middle button on the front of her blouse was missing. She pulled the gap together and her face, under its grime, reddened. Jeremy stared up into the nearest tree.

''My mother can sew that on for you, if you like,'' he offered.

Then he remembered that Mum was in Hamilton at the hospital. She had said she would try to be back by

the time they got home, but he had had the feeling that
she doubted she would make it.

Tess gave him a scornful glance.

"I can sew on my own buttons, for Pete's sake. I'd just
rather Grandpa didn't see me looking like such a mess.
Grandma was always at me to act like a lady and now
that she's dead, Grandpa thinks he has to keep up the
good work."

She gave a short, self-conscious laugh. Before he could
stop himself, Jeremy chuckled, too. Tess a lady! That
would be the day.

"Maybe he won't be home," he said. It sounded lame
but it was the only thing he could think of.

Tess's face brightened.

"You're right. This is the day he works at the apartment building next door. If I hurry, I can get changed
before he comes in."

She started walking. Jeremy felt he had to walk along
with her, whether he wanted to or not. His good manners had him trapped. Tess, although she had said she
had to hurry, sauntered so that he could keep up. Neither of them said anything further. He was glad they
didn't see anyone he knew.

Soon they were at the end of the Talbots' driveway.
She stopped. He was surprised that she knew where he
lived. There was a pause while he shifted from one foot
to the other and wondered how to get away. Then he
turned and took off.

"So long," he tossed back over his shoulder.

She made no answer. He had broken into a trot but he
halted to look back in spite of himself. She was already
almost out of sight.

Feeling foolish and deflated, Jeremy went up the steps to his own front door. He had been right all along. Who'd want to be friends with a girl, anyway, especially a weird, snooty girl like that?

Fourteen

Mum wasn't home. Neither was Sarah. To punish him for being away for most of the day, Blue ignored him for five whole minutes. Even after she had acknowledged his presence with an aloof gaze, she kept her distance. She forgave him utterly only when he sat down on the floor and began throwing a twist of paper for her to chase.

Jeremy didn't like coming into the empty house. He was used to hearing his mother call a greeting the minute he opened the door. Oh, she had been out sometimes, of course, but this was different.

Leaving Blue to her own devices, he scrambled to his feet and went in search of a snack. As he bit into his third cookie, Sarah arrived.

''Guess what? I'm the best reader in my class,'' she bragged, her cheeks pink, her eyes bright.

"Who says so?"

She refused to be squelched.

"I got *three* gold stars."

Jeremy remembered those gold stars. They were special. He saw her glance fly around the kitchen, automatically searching for Mum.

He spoke quickly.

"Pretty fair. Pretty fair for a pipsqueak."

When Mum finally did come, they all went out for fish and chips. Sarah talked a blue streak. When she ran out of steam at last, Mum asked how his day had gone. He had been waiting for this moment. He poured out the story of the calico cat's rescue. Both Mum and Sarah were shocked at what the bullies had done; both were impressed by the dramatic way Tess and he had saved it.

"Good for you, Jeremy," his mother said.

Had Dad told her about their talk about Tess? Probably. He hoped she wasn't getting the wrong idea. He was glad he had helped Tess out, but that did not mean they were friends.

Once that first schoolday was over, Mum started staying with Dad into the evening. Mrs. Barr either came from next door to take charge or had them to her house for supper. At first she waited to see Sarah safely into bed. Then Jeremy, catching a resentful look on his sister's face, offered to take over. Mum talked to Sarah and decided to give it a try. Sarah enjoyed the new arrangement. Although Jeremy did order her around, he wasn't fussy about her washing behind her ears or flossing her teeth. He also sometimes let her stay up later than Mum would have done, getting small favours from her in return.

Then Mum surprised them one night by coming home

in time for supper. There was a feeling of celebration among the three of them as they sat down together. Sarah especially had a lot to say, since she had usually been in bed by the time her mother arrived home at night. Jeremy was content to listen. He really had nothing special or different to talk about. He had made no new friends and school was the same old drag. He had already told her how much he liked Mr. Darling.

They were having dessert when Sarah asked, ''When is Daddy coming home?''

''Oh, I almost forgot. He sent you something.'' Mum sprang up and went to her bag.

Jeremy was not surprised when she returned with a package of licorice. Everybody knew licorice was Sarah's favourite thing.

''He bought them from the cart they wheel around at the hospital,'' Mum said.

Sarah was so eager to begin on the candy that she didn't notice that her mother had not answered her question. Jeremy looked at his mother searchingly. She glanced at him and then looked away.

''What did he send Jeremy?'' Sarah demanded, her words indistinct because she had stuffed two pieces into her mouth at once.

''The licorice is for him, too, greedy,'' Mum laughed. ''He did send home a paperback he has just finished rereading that he thinks you'll like, Jeremy. I'll get it for you later.''

Sarah was in bed and he was in his pajamas when she came to his room. She had a copy of *Kim* in her hand. She sat down next to him on the edge of the bed and reached out to stroke Blue. Blue usually did not appreciate petting unless she had been the one to invite it, but this time she obligingly rolled over onto her back so that Mum could rub her belly.

"I don't know if what I'm going to do is the right thing or not, Jeremy," Mum said, her eyes fixed on the little cat. "Your dad and I talked it over and we thought you have a right to know . . ."

Jeremy felt a coldness start somewhere deep inside him. He wanted to stop her before she said anything more. He knew that it was something he did not want to hear, something he already knew in some corner of his mind, something he could not face. He did not move or speak.

His mother took a deep breath and went steadily on.

"He is not going to get well. Perhaps you have already guessed. You must have seen that he was much worse even before he left here. There isn't anything anyone can do. Nobody knows exactly how long he will live but he won't be coming home from the hospital. He needs injections often now . . ."

She had been talking faster and faster as if she wanted to get it over with. Now she stopped and looked straight at him. She was not crying but he knew she was close to it. He hoped against hope that she wouldn't cry. It was enough of a nightmare as it was. He could not think of anything to say. He could not think of what to think, even. He felt as though his brain had gone into slow motion.

"I . . . I . . . how is he?" he stammered. "I mean . . . is he . . . I don't know what I mean."

"He's tired and weak and in quite a bit of pain at times, but he is still himself," she answered. "I've been reading to him. We finished *Kim* today. He thinks you'll like it. I feel it is too old for you but he says you'll grow up to it.''

Those words, which he had heard his father say before about other books, brought Dad into the room with them. Dad had given him *Who Has Seen the Wind* and *The Snow Goose* and *Eagle of the Ninth*. Last spring the two of them had read together all five books of Susan Cooper's *The Dark Is Rising*. He had loved those. Dad liked long books, books you could ''get your teeth into.'' Jeremy liked them, too.

He's dying. Dad's dying, he said inside his head. He couldn't believe it. He wouldn't believe it.

''I don't know what to say,'' he mumbled miserably.

Mum put her hands over her face for a moment and, as suddenly, dropped them clasped onto her lap again.

''You don't have to say anything,'' she told him, her voice uneven, as though the words were catching on something. ''I told Dad how much you've been helping with Sarah and he said to tell you he's proud of you. I'm not going to tell her yet. She's too little. But we both thought . . . you should know.''

''I'll read the book,'' he promised, knowing it did not matter whether he read it or not.

Then, without another word, he was in his mother's arms, hugged up close against her, and they were crying together.

Fifteen

Jeremy dawdled over getting dressed the next morning. He didn't want to face his mother. Would she expect him to say something about what she had told him? There was nothing he could say. As he took his place at the table, ducking his head low over his oatmeal, he felt strange, as though he had someone else's clothes on, clothes stiff with newness and a little too tight. When he shot his mother a swift, embarrassed glance, she smiled at him and went right back to reading the paper. Maybe she didn't know what to say, either.

He was glad it was Saturday.

He finished his porridge, set the bowl aside and looked at Sarah. She was intent on making islands in her oatmeal. He sat watching her, remembering when he had liked doing that. She raised her head, caught him at it and glowered.

"Jeremy, quit looking at me like that!"

"Like what?" he returned, continuing to look at her.

"Mummy, make Jeremy stop looking at me that way," his sister demanded.

Mum usually ignored their bickering, but this time she said firmly, "Your porridge is to be eaten, not played with, Sarah. It must be stone cold by now."

"I like it cold," Sarah pouted, "and Jeremy shouldn't . . ."

"Your brother is not looking at you any longer," Mum said with a smile. "He's looking at me. Sarah, make Jeremy stop looking at me like that!"

Her exact imitation of Sarah's whine made even Sarah laugh. Jeremy grinned and then stiffened. How could he smile? Misery washed over him. He bunched up his shoulders, trying to fend it off.

"Stop slumping, Jeremy. Sit up straight."

These ordinary words seemed to put the ground back under his feet. He made himself a piece of toast. It was good, as good as the piece he had had yesterday morning. This comforted him for a moment and then saddened him, although he did not know why. He gobbled the last couple of bites and stood up.

"Excuse me. I'm meeting some guys."

"Have a good time," his mother said, just as she did every day, and Sarah chimed in, just as she always did, "What are you going to do? Can I come?"

"Not a chance," he told her.

Giving Blue a farewell pat, he left the house. He had no plans, really. He jogged down the street to the nearby park.

Some kids he didn't know were playing touch football there. He hung around watching for fifteen minutes and finally they let him play, too. He was glad to be running hard and yelling, glad he didn't really know any of the boys. None of them even asked him his name.

At lunch Sarah gave Mum three drawings to send to Dad. Jeremy had to admit that she was good at drawing. The arms on the people were too short and their noses too pointed and their feet were a bit peculiar but they still looked alive. Mum especially liked one of a whole bunch of kids roller-skating. One little boy was flat on his bottom, his legs in the air, and two others had run into each other. Just looking at it made you laugh.

"Your dad will love this one," Mum said.

Jeremy wondered for a split second if the conversation they had had the night before had all been a dream. Mum sounded so calm, so ordinary. If what she had told him had been true, wouldn't she be crying? Then he remembered that she had cried and that Sarah didn't know. That was why Mum had to pretend.

"I like that one best, too," he said, trying to speak as normally as she did.

He found that pretending helped. It pushed the unreal, the unbelievable sadness away. Even if you couldn't forget it, you didn't have to talk about it.

"Aren't you going to send Daddy anything, Jeremy?" Sarah asked. She sounded smug.

He scowled at her. He wasn't any good at art. Boy, she was a drip.

"Jeremy already sent Hoot," his mother said quietly. "Your father keeps him on the table right next to his bed. Now, Sarah, before I go, I want you to help me tidy up the mess in your room."

When Mum left for Hamilton, Jeremy went to the bicycle repair shop. He paid for his bike and rode away on it. Sarah was over at Mrs. Barr's. He had nothing planned. It was good, though, just having his bike back. He had not ridden on it all summer. He wheeled up one street and down another. If only the twins were still here! The three of them could go on a bike hike. They could take hot dogs and build a fire and sit and talk.

Suddenly he knew that was what he wanted to do. He needed someone to talk to.

Without exactly planning to, he found himself heading for Tess Medford's house. He was pretty sure he knew where she lived, although he had never been there. Charles Street, that was it. He thought the house was somewhere in this block. He pedalled more slowly, looking. What had she said about her grandfather working in an apartment building next door? Well, there was an apartment building. It was on the corner. There was only one house next to it. Tess was nowhere in sight.

He speeded up, pretending he had not been searching for the house at all. It had been a dumb idea. Yet, when he was a couple of blocks away, he turned the handlebars and circled back. Maybe this time he would see her. Then, as he was riding past for the third time, she came out with some letters to mail.

She spotted him at once. He saw her hesitate for an instant and then walk on. He pedalled up and braked to a stop.

''Hi,'' he said casually.

She halted, turned to face him and waited. She was still some distance away from him.

''Rescued any cats lately?'' he asked.

She looked surprised and then she smiled. She started walking over the grass toward him.

"Not lately," she said, sounding shy. "How about you?"

"Me, neither." Then, for something to say, he added, "I have a cat at home, though. Her name's Blue."

"Why?"

"Because she *is* blue," he said impatiently. "Well, sort of silvery blue and charcoal blue on her face and legs and tail. Her eyes are blue, too. She's part Siamese."

"Oh," Tess said.

Jeremy did not wait for her to think of something else to say about cats. He looked away from her and burst out, "You were right. About my dad, I mean. He's not going to get better."

After a long silence, Tess said slowly, "You mean . . . he's . . ."

She could not finish the sentence. Jeremy sat, his hands gripping the handlebars so tightly his knuckles were white, his gaze fixed on the road. Then, when he remained silent, she swallowed hard, took a run at it and got the whole thing out in the open between them.

"You mean, he's dying?"

"Yeah," Jeremy said, relieved that he had not had to say it. "Mum told me last night. Sarah doesn't know. I can't . . . I can't believe it, really."

Tess came a step nearer to him. He flashed a glance at her and saw his own disbelief and sorrow mirrored in her eyes. All at once, he knew why he had come to find her. She had been the one person he could think of who would understand. She had spoken herself of her grandmother's death and her parents. . . . Something must have happened to her parents.

"Did your parents die?" he asked in a low voice.

He didn't think he was being nosy like Mrs. Meigs. He felt he had to know. But Tess's answer shocked him.

"No," she said flatly. She gave a bitter little laugh and added, "Not that I know of, anyway."

Did she think he was snooping? Out of the corner of his eye he saw her scuff up some fallen leaves with the toe of her shoe. Neither of them spoke for at least a minute.

"Well, I guess I'd better get going," he began, straightening up his bike and putting his foot on the pedal.

"I don't mind your asking about it." Tess was staring off down the street. "I don't want to talk about it but I don't mind your asking. And I'm really sorry about . . . about your father."

"Thanks," he said, not knowing how else to reply.

As he shoved off from the curb, he looked back and saw her still standing there, watching him go. She gave a suggestion of a wave but dropped her hand at once.

"So long," he called back to her.

"So long," she said.

He rode around town most of the afternoon, giving himself up to the feeling of power as he shifted gears and went coasting down one hill and pumping up the next. He enjoyed the wind cooling his cheeks and tousling his hair. He zoomed around corners and zigzagged every so often when there was no traffic. He sought out the steepest, longest hill in town and swooped down it, pretending he was riding a rollercoaster. It was not so hard to keep from thinking.

When his mother came home, Sarah and he were in their pajamas, both immersed in comic books. Sarah jumped up and ran to meet Mum at the door.

''Did Daddy like my pictures?''

''Of course he did. His favourite was the same as mine, the one of the kids skating.''

Jeremy took a deep breath. He looked right at Mum and did his best to keep his voice steady.

''How was he?'' he asked.

Then he braced himself for the answer. Mum took him entirely by surprise, however, when she said, ''You'll see for yourself tomorrow. I'm going to take the two of you with me to visit him.''

Sixteen

T he next afternoon when they were on their way to Hamilton, Sarah said, ''I thought kids weren't allowed in. You've never taken us before.''

''They do let them in on Sundays,'' her mother explained. ''I could have taken you last week. But he's not well enough to have you stay all afternoon. Besides, you'd be bored. Today Margery is coming from London so we'll only stay for a few minutes and leave the rest of the time for her.''

Jeremy was looking out the window. He was scared. Did a person who was dying look different somehow? He shivered.

When they went into the hospital, Jeremy sniffed in that special smell that hospitals have. They had to rush to catch the elevator. Then, before he was ready, they were inside Dad's room. A nurse and a doctor were standing by the bed.

Mum, Jeremy and Sarah waited by the door. Jeremy stole a glance at his father. He was filled with relief to see that Dad still looked like Dad. Thinner. More tired. But the smile he sent them was his own smile.

As the doctor and nurse turned to leave, Aunt Margery arrived. Jeremy went up to the bed to kiss his father but Sarah was already pushing past him. He got out of her way. Dad hugged Sarah and then looked past her and held out his hand. He was smiling right at Jeremy.

"Have you started *Kim* yet?" his father asked.

Jeremy hadn't. There hadn't really been time. He opened his mouth to explain and then gave up.

"I will as soon as I get home," he promised. He heard his voice sounding forced. If only he had thought to begin on the book last night . . .

Dad had a box of chocolates that he passed around. Sarah, getting one with a cherry inside, spat it out indignantly. Everyone laughed.

Aunt Margery began to talk about the traffic on her way from London. She had had to drive through a rainstorm. The conversation moved to a discussion of the weather. Jeremy shifted his weight from one foot to the other.

Then, before he had managed to say anything that held meaning, he heard Mum saying it was time for them to go.

"You can only take so much company when you're in the hospital, even such special visitors as we are," she said lightly.

"But I have company even when you're not here," Dad told her. Reaching out his hand, he picked up Hoot.

That one moment made the whole visit worthwhile.

Sarah fell asleep on the drive home. After looking down

to make sure she really was sleeping, Mum said quietly, "It's hard to be yourself in an unnatural setting like that. We'll go again next Sunday. I know he wants to have a real talk with you. I can take Sarah to the tuck shop and give you two some time to yourselves."

That night, Jeremy tackled *Kim*. It was a long book with small print and it was hard to get into. But Dad had taught him not to give up until he had read at least three chapters in a book. The opening sentence was good: "He sat, in defiance of municipal orders, astride the gun . . ."

But then the foreign words began cropping up and he wondered if Dad had made a mistake this time. The first chapter was twenty-four pages long. Maybe thirty pages of such small print would be the same as three chapters in a normal book. Then he got caught up in the story and forgot to keep track.

Kim was an orphan boy who lived in India. He looked Indian but it turned out that his father had been a British soldier. He spent most of the book having exciting adventures as he travelled all over the country acting as a sort of spy for the government, and looking after an old holy man who was seeking a mysterious river.

Jeremy took the book to school the next day. Kim Chiong was pleased to learn a book had been named after him but he was not interested in reading it. Jeremy was glad. It seemed private, not something to share. He read it every spare moment. Sometimes it was complicated and hard to follow. It had far too many long descriptions and not enough talking. But Jeremy didn't really mind. He wanted to do something difficult for Dad. He did skip quite a lot. The sentences were so long and there were so many words he didn't understand. But before long, he would find Kim up to his ears in another breathtaking escapade.

Jeremy finished the book in less than a week. The ending disappointed him. What was the old man talking about? Could that little stream really have been the river he was looking for?

I'll ask Dad, he thought.

Then it was as though he had run full tilt into a stone wall. Ask Dad? When? It wasn't something you could talk about when you were visiting someone in a hospital, not with Sarah there, too. Even if Mum took Sarah to the tuck shop the way she had said, it would take more than a few minutes. And Dad wasn't coming home.

Jeremy sat, staring blindly at the world beyond his sunlit window. Forget it. Forget it, said a dull voice inside his head.

He got up and, going into the living room, shoved *Kim* into the first space he saw in the bookshelf. Then he turned on the TV.

The next Sunday, Dad was not well enough to have visitors. He had been having some kind of treatment and Mum came home on Saturday night looking tired, and said they would not be able to go. Before he could stop himself, Jeremy felt relieved. What was the matter with him?

''He asked if you had finished reading *Kim*,'' Mum said.

''Oh . . . yeah, I did,'' Jeremy answered, not meeting her gaze. ''I'll write him a letter and you can take it to him.''

But the next day when she left, he had no note ready. He had not known what to write. She didn't say anything but he could tell she was disappointed. Two minutes after she had gone, he had slapped Sarah and yelled at Blue. It was a rotten day all around.

Then, after school on Monday, when he came sprinting across the lawn to the house, he saw that Blue was not sitting in the window in her usual spot. Was she mad at him? He opened the door and called her name.

No Blue appeared but Sarah came running in at the back door. She was crying.

"Where's Blue?" he demanded, ignoring her tears.

"She's lost!" Sarah wailed, her words punctuated by noisy sobs. "I got out early and when I opened the door, I was in a hurry because I had to go to the bathroom . . ."

"You let her *out*?" Jeremy yelled.

"Not on purpose. She just ran past me somehow. I called her and called her but she didn't come. And I've looked and looked but I can't find her anywhere!"

Sarah's voice rose. She was growing hysterical. He'd get nowhere until he calmed her down. He fought to keep his self-control. Putting one hand on her shoulder, he gave her a not-ungentle shake.

"Quit that!" he told her sternly. "That won't help. Here. Blow your nose."

He waited while she did it, trying to keep from her his own rising panic. When she was quieter, he went on.

"Did you see her at all after she got out? Think. Which way did she go?"

"I don't know. She was just gone! Oh, here comes Mrs. Barr. Maybe she saw."

In no time flat, Mrs. Barr had organized three search parties. She got Rodney, the boy who had just delivered her groceries, to go with Sarah back toward the school. She sent Jeremy to search in the park. And she got into her car to drive around and hunt up and down the nearby streets. They were all to report back in half an hour.

"Blue! Blue! Here, Puss-puss," Jeremy called.

He went slowly, looking carefully behind each tree, bush or big rock. Blue was still a small cat, and she loved playing hide-and-seek. She might be sitting somewhere watching him right now and keeping extra quiet, waiting for him to find her. Or she could have gone some other way and, this very minute, was being crushed under the wheels of a truck.

"Blue!" he called again, trying hard to keep exasperation and fear out of his voice. "Oh, Blue, come on, please!"

Half an hour went past. Suppose he turned his head too quickly and missed her? Suppose some kid thought she was a stray and took her home? Would she go with anyone else? He didn't think so but how could he be sure? Could she possibly be up a tree?

He turned to go home, breaking into a run, praying that one of the others had her there safe and sound. Mrs. Barr was on the front walk.

"I couldn't find her," she called out so that he wouldn't begin to hope. "The others aren't back yet."

He went up to her.

"I'll check the park again," he said. "I could have missed her."

"Wait," Mrs. Barr said, putting her hand on his arm. "They may have spotted her somewhere and be needing you to come and coax her down . . ."

The phone rang inside the house.

"I'll get it." He ran inside and picked up the phone.

"Jeremy," said Tess Medford's voice, "this probably sounds dumb, but is that blue cat of yours missing?"

Seventeen

Jeremy gasped.

"Yes. We've been hunting all over for her."

"I thought this cat looked like the one you said was yours," Tess said excitedly. "I saw her going by on the sidewalk and I'd never seen her around here before. I've got her here now."

Jeremy could hardly speak. He took a deep breath and called to Mrs. Barr who had followed him as far as the front door.

"It's one of the kids in my class, Tess Medford. She's got Blue." Then he spoke into the phone again. "I'll be right over."

"I'll bring her part way," Tess offered. "I think she likes me."

"Are you positive it's Blue?" Jeremy asked, trying to ward off possible disappointment.

There was a pause. "Yes," Tess was gruff with embarrassment. "I've seen her waiting for you in your front window."

Tess was only a third of the way when he met her. She had not hurried because she was carrying Blue in her arms. Jeremy took her and somehow managed to stroke, hug and scold her all at the same time.

Then he remembered his manners.

"Thanks a lot!" he said, looking at Tess over Blue's head. "I really like this dumb cat."

Tess smiled and turned to go. Something made him ask, to his own surprise, "Would you like to come over to my place for awhile? Mum's not home but she doesn't mind if we ask people in. We could watch TV or . . . or something."

Tess did not answer for a moment. Her eyes seemed to search his face. He did his best to look welcoming. After all, she had found Blue for him. She hesitated one second longer and then raised her head.

"Sure." The two of them walked side by side in a friendly silence.

Sarah was in front of the house playing hopscotch with some friends. As Jeremy and Tess drew near, she called to them, "We're eating at the Barrs' tonight. Mr. Barr is going to barbecue. We can have hamburgers or hot dogs, whichever we want."

Mrs. Barr, hearing her, leaned out the kitchen door. She smiled when she saw Blue safe in Jeremy's arms.

"Would your friend like to stay for supper? There's plenty of food and she'd be welcome."

Jeremy was taken aback. He turned to Tess. She looked surprised, too, but she answered calmly enough.

"Grandpa's out tonight so I was just going to make myself a sandwich. If you're sure it's no . . ."

"I'll give a shout when it's ready," Mrs. Barr said. "It won't be for at least half an hour."

"Come over to our house," Jeremy invited. "I have to take Blue home, anyway. We'd be safe there from this kindergarten mob."

Tess followed him obediently. Once inside the door, he put Blue down. When Tess seated herself in the easy chair by the window, the cat jumped up on the arm of it and butted her head up under Tess's chin.

"She must like you," Jeremy said. "She ignores most strangers."

Tess held her fingers out and Blue rubbed the side of her head against them.

Jeremy went and got a paper bag so that Blue could show off. Before long, Tess was laughing out loud. It seemed only minutes before Sarah came running to tell them supper was ready.

They were still eating when Jeremy, looking out the window, saw Mum's car pull into the Talbots' driveway. Sarah, hearing the car door shut, looked over her shoulder, saw the car and started sliding off her chair.

"You stay where you are," Mrs. Barr said, putting a restraining hand on her shoulder. "You've hardly started your supper. Your mother will know you're over here. Will she want a hot dog or a hamburger, do you think?"

"She likes both," Sarah said, staying where she was.

"Put a hamburger on for her, Albert," Mrs. Barr ordered.

Jeremy was pleased that his mother was going to meet Tess. She'd be sure to tell Dad about it tomorrow. In his mind's eye, he could see clearly the smile that would light up his father's face. Dad would imagine, of course, that he had changed his mind about making friends with Tess and that wasn't exactly true, though she was a lot better than he had imagined. The news was going to mean more to Dad than a bunch of Sarah's dopey drawings.

Mum was taking a long time coming. Nobody said anything until her hamburger was ready. Then Mrs. Barr clucked her tongue disapprovingly.

"We shouldn't have cooked it so soon," she fussed.

Jeremy put down the ketchup bottle carefully. Tess had stopped eating. Sarah was fidgeting. Why didn't Mum hurry up and get here? She'd had enough time to have an entire bath.

He looked at Tess. Their eyes met. Abruptly he shoved his chair back.

"I'll go see," he said. "I'll be right back."

He was out the door before they could stop him. He didn't run. Mum didn't usually get back until eight or eight-thirty. He looked up at the sky. It was getting darker earlier now. Well, it would soon be Hallowe'en. It was always dark after supper on Hallowe'en night. Then he was at the back door.

He opened it quietly and slipped inside. His mother wasn't in the kitchen or the living room. He could hear no sound anywhere. Then he saw that her bedroom door was closed.

He stood there staring at it. Should he knock? Or should he just go away and pretend he hadn't been there?

Blue came out from behind the couch and wove around his feet. He leaned down and picked her up.

"Hello, Blue-cat." His voice sounded husky, as if he hadn't used it for a long time. He cleared his throat.

"Jeremy, is that you?" Mum called. She didn't open the door.

"Yeah. Mrs. Barr said to tell you she's got your supper over there."

"Jeremy," she said again, as if she needed to say his name, "would you go back and tell her thank you but I'm not hungry. As soon as you're finished eating, bring Sarah and come right home. I'll be waiting. Okay?"

"Okay." He didn't want to go. She was having trouble with her voice, too.

Squatting down, he set Blue gently on the floor. He stroked her once and then said, too softly for his mother to hear, "Take care of things, Blue."

When he straightened up, he did not hesitate any longer. He went quickly back across the yard and into the Barrs' kitchen.

"She's not hungry," he said. "I guess she got something at the hospital. She wants us to go home when we're done."

"I'm finished now," Sarah said brightly, starting to get off her chair.

"You have to wait for me," Jeremy said in a firm voice. "She said you have to wait for me."

He sat down and began stuffing the rest of his supper into his mouth. He didn't take time to chew. He just gulped it down with swallows of milk. He pretended he didn't see Sarah scowling at him. He had forgotten Tess entirely. Mrs. Barr was over at the counter cutting a slice of cake for his mother. She put plastic wrap over the cake and brought it to Jeremy.

"She may say she's not hungry but she's probably just too tired to eat," she said fussily. "You get her to eat it when she's had time to put her feet up. Did she say there was anything I could do?"

Jeremy's mouth was full. He gave a big swallow and coughed. Mr. Barr reached out and tapped him on the back.

"No, she just said to say thank you and she'd see you later," he answered.

Then Tess rose and pushed back her chair.

"I'd like to thank you, too, Mrs. Barr," she said politely. "I guess I'd better go now. Grandpa might come home and wonder where I am."

A moment later, she was at the door, pulling on her jacket. Jeremy looked at her plate. She had left the last few bites of cake. She gave a small wave of her hand, a little like a salute.

"So long, Jeremy," she said and slipped away.

"I'm done," he said, getting up from the table. "Thanks a lot, Mrs. Barr. Okay, Sarah, let's go."

As she began to dash past him, he caught her by the shoulder. She glared up at him. He had no idea what to say to make her walk with him. He was surprised when his words came out lightly, jokingly.

"You've been out for dinner. You're always playing you're Lady Somebody-or-other. So take my arm, Princess."

He bowed, offering her his arm. Always delighted to play-act, she took it with a little curtsey. As he held the back door open for her, he was even laughing.

Mum was waiting for them in the kitchen. Her face told them something was terribly wrong before she said a word. Sarah was the one to break the silence.

"What's the matter?" she said, her voice shrill with alarm.

Mum pulled out the chair nearest to her, sat down and reached out to them.

"Your father's dead. Adrian's dead. He died at three o'clock this afternoon."

Eighteen

*E*ven though he had been almost expecting it, Jeremy could not believe that Mum was telling the truth when she said Dad had died. He could see that she didn't believe it, either. Sarah, frightened more by the look on Mum's face than by what she had said, started to cry. Melly Talbot hugged her and said, "Don't, Sarah. Hush." But not as if she were really aware of Sarah's tears.

Still with her arm around the little girl, she began to talk again. Jeremy tried to concentrate.

"The doctor said it was a blessing. It was very sudden. One minute we were talking. The next, he was gone . . . gone."

Jeremy felt he should do something for her. Did listening count? She was talking again. She didn't seem to be able to stop.

"The doctor wanted to send someone with me. But I knew I could drive home all right and I didn't want to be with some stranger. He called the funeral home for me before I left . . . I ought to . . . there are things I have to do. I must get through to Margery.'' Her voice faltered.

''Sure,'' Jeremy found himself saying. ''Sarah and I can watch TV. You don't have to worry about us. We're okay.''

What a dumb thing to say! His mother reached out her hand to him. It was as if she were drowning and he had thrown her a rope. She held onto his hand tightly for a moment.

''Thank you, Jeremy. Mrs. Barr . . . she won't be coming over, will she? Did she guess?''

He shook his head.

''She sent you a piece of cake.'' He showed her the plate in his free hand. When she looked at it vaguely, he set it on the table. Sarah, still within the circle of his mother's arm, was now sniffling quietly. Jeremy gently pried her loose and, putting his arm around her shoulders, led her away to the television.

''Why don't you phone Aunt Margery now?'' he said to his mother over his shoulder. In that moment, she was the child, he the grown-up. He heard her rise obediently, cross to the telephone and start to dial.

Good. Aunt Margery would take over. He had done all right so far but he was sure he could not keep it up.

''Don't cry, Sarah,'' he said in a voice exactly like his father's. ''You get to choose the channel.''

They sat side by side on the couch. Usually whoever got there first hogged the whole couch while the other sat in the captain's chair. More often than not, Jeremy, being bigger and quicker at seizing his chance, took over the couch and stretched out to watch in complete comfort. Now, however, they not only sat together but they sat up straight. Sarah didn't even take off her shoes. That was always the first thing she did when she plunked herself down in front of the set.

It was queer to be watching a rerun of an old Muppet show and not laughing. It was queer still when, forgetting for a moment what had happened, Jeremy suddenly realized he was laughing and so was Sarah. He felt ashamed. He opened his mouth to tell her to stop and then did not tell her after all. It was better if she did forget. Then, without saying a word, she pressed close to him and shivered. She, too, had remembered.

He made himself sit back and say, "Which one do you like best?"

"Kermit," Sarah said at once, leaning against him. He felt her relax. Soon she was laughing once more.

When the show ended, he chose one he knew she would like. Over the sound of the television, he heard his mother answering the door, voices murmuring, feet coming and going. He glimpsed the minister in the hall and a little later caught sight of Mrs. Barr. Then he got interested in the show and sat forward, engrossed in spite of himself.

After what seemed a long time, Mum came to take Sarah to bed. Jeremy went with them. There were people looking at them as they crossed the hall and he was glad when Mum shut Sarah's door.

As she tried to talk with them but couldn't at first, he knew that it was true that his father had died. He knew it but it still seemed unreal. He wasn't even terribly sad. He wondered if there was something wrong with him. His mother looked up at him over the top of Sarah's head.

"Jeremy," she said unsteadily, "what sits at the bottom of the sea and shakes?"

He could feel his eyes stretching wide, his lips parting in surprise. Had she gone crazy?

"I don't know. What?" he said automatically.

"A nervous wreck."

Then all three of them were laughing. He laughed so hard that his stomach hurt and tears poured down his cheeks. It wasn't all that funny but he couldn't stop himself.

"I know one," Sarah said. "Why didn't they play cards on the Ark?"

Jeremy had known that one for years but he decided not to spoil it for her.

"Why?" Mum said.

"Because Noah was always standing on the pack."

"On the deck, dummy," he corrected her.

"That's what I said, dummy," his sister snapped.

He was about to argue but Mum shook her head slightly and he subsided. He had a riddle of his own to try.

"What goes, 'Ha, ha, ha, plop,' " he asked.

They couldn't guess.

"Someone laughing his head off," he grinned.

"Yuck!" Sarah said but she giggled in spite of herself. Mum groaned.

"That's enough of that. We could never top that one. Choose a book, Sarah."

Jeremy stayed to listen. He did not want to be by himself. When Mum finished, Sarah begged for another story. This time, Mum took turns reading pages with her. Jeremy remembered when she had had him doing that. He wondered if he had needed as much help as Sarah seemed to. In his memory, he read flawlessly.

"Mummy, *read*!" he heard his sister say suddenly.

But Mum didn't. Jeremy glanced at her and saw her face bunched up. She looked exactly the way Sarah did when she was fighting not to cry.

"It's my turn," he said, grabbing the book. "How come you never let me take a turn, sissy?"

"Don't call me sissy," Sarah protested, forgetting Mum's silence in her indignation.

"But you *are* my sister," he said, pretending innocence. "It just means . . ."

"I don't care!" she yelled. "Mum, make him stop saying 'sissy' to me."

Mum, herself again, gave Sarah a little squeeze.

"Perhaps his feelings are hurt because we didn't invite him to read," she said with a smile.

"Go ahead and read then, boysie-baby," Sarah flung at him.

She looked so proud of this sally that both he and Mum laughed.

It was time to turn out the light. Jeremy checked his watch. It was twenty to ten! Sarah was supposed to have her light out by eight. Even so, as he and Mum were about to leave the room, Sarah reached out and grabbed hold of her mother's hand.

"Mummy, stay till I go to sleep," she said, her voice wobbling.

Jeremy felt her panic inside himself. He swallowed and stiffened his shoulders. He was glad he had already flipped the switch so the only light came in through the door he now held open. Mum hesitated.

"It's late, sweetheart," she said gently, "and I want to see Jeremy into bed tonight, too, even though he is practically grown up."

Sarah didn't argue. She rolled over so that her back was turned to them. But Jeremy knew she had started to cry.

"It's okay. I have something to do for school," he said, giving the first excuse which came to his mind.

"You won't have to go to school tomorrow," Mum told him.

"We're having a test next week on the Prairies so I have to study anyway."

"I thought you just had a test on the Prairies."

Why did she have to remember that? Should he go on with the lie? Then, before he got in deeper, he realized she had stopped quizzing him and was sitting back down on the edge of Sarah's bed. She began singing softly. He left.

He tiptoed down the hall to his own room. He did not turn on the light or get out his books. He undressed quickly in the dark and got right into bed without washing his face or brushing his teeth. Usually, once he was in bed, he felt safe and snug, the way he imagined birds felt in their nests. Tonight he only felt alone. He remembered feeling like this the first time he had gone to camp. They had called it homesickness. But how could you be homesick when you were in your very own bed?

He began to count, running the string of numbers through the lonely emptiness.

One thousand and one . . . one thousand and two . . .

Every time he reached one thousand and ten, he backed up and began over. Doing that had sometimes helped at camp. It soothed him now, too. He could feel himself moving further and further away from the thoughts and feelings that were pushing in upon him.

He must have dozed because the next thing he knew, his mother was bending over him. He lay absolutely still and kept on breathing slowly and evenly, as if he were sound asleep.

"Is he awake?" someone whispered from the doorway.

It sounded like Aunt Margery. Could she be here already? He didn't want Aunt Margery looking at him. He stayed still.

Mum didn't answer his aunt's question. She put something down on his bedside table, stood there for another long minute and then quietly left the room. As she crossed to the door he felt furious at her all at once. How could she think he was asleep? She should have stayed with him and made Aunt Margery go away.

Then he took in the fact that Mum had not answered Aunt Margery. Maybe she did know. Maybe she thought he wanted her to go away.

Then he remembered that Mum had put something on his bedside table. He reached out cautiously in the darkness and groped for it.

It was Hoot.

The minute his fingers recognized the small stone owl, he jerked his hand back as if it had burned him. The calm he had been building up so carefully shattered. His breath came in ragged gasps. His hands tightened into fists. He was alone and his father was gone.

Alone. Gone.

The words went echoing around inside his head. Then Blue jumped squarely on top of him. She was purring like a locomotive. Gasping, with relief this time, he sat up and took her in his arms. For once she didn't twist free but stayed where she was, her purr growing even louder.

"Oh, Blue, Blue," he said, burying his face in her soft fur.

She licked his cheek, her tongue rough as sandpaper. Remembering how she hated being held tightly, he let her go and lay back down. She curled up next to him. The warmth of her and her contented, rumbling purr comforted him more than anything had that day. After a minute, he stretched out his hand and picked up Hoot. Closing his fingers around the owl, he rested his hot cheek against it and let sleep come.

Nineteen

The next day was Tuesday, but it didn't feel like it. People kept coming and going and they were all quiet and serious. Neighbours and friends brought food, more food than the Talbots could eat in a week. Jeremy felt as if he were in the way most of the time, as if he were visiting in somebody else's house. He hated it.

Mum and Aunt Margery went to the funeral home in the afternoon and again in the evening. Once the dishes were done and their beds were made, he and Sarah spent most of the day in front of the television. Yet Jeremy never got to see a whole program through. He was too busy keeping Blue from going out the front door each time a visitor came in.

He had never been so relieved to see a day draw to its close. Mum came home in time to put Sarah to bed. She called him to come, too.

"Your father's funeral will be tomorrow afternoon," Mum said. "Margery thinks that children should not be taken to funerals and, if you don't want to go, that's fine. I'm not sure what it will mean to you if you do go. It won't be easy. Mrs. Barr would be glad to have you over there if you'd rather stay home."

She sounded unsure, not like herself. Jeremy thought she wished them to go but didn't want to make them do so. He looked over at Sarah. Meeting her eyes, he knew they felt the same way about it.

"I'd like to go," he said.

"So would I," Sarah said.

Jeremy made himself smile at his mother.

"It'll be okay. You'll see."

On their way into the funeral home, Mum was walking between them and holding Sarah's hand. She had not held his hand in public for a long time. Yet right then he wanted her to and suddenly it came to him that he was old enough now to take her hand, not because he needed to cling to her but because he knew she needed him to be close. When she felt his fingers curl around hers, Mum glanced down at him and, as quickly, looked away. She kept her head high and her shoulders straight. But their fingers stayed locked from that instant.

The room seemed to be full of strangers. They either hastily looked away or they stared at his mother as the three Talbots came in. The air seemed heavy with the fragrance of flowers.

Throughout the time there, he felt as though he were acting in a play. He didn't have a big part but it was important that he do it properly. He had to concentrate hard on doing the right thing at the right time. The smell of so many flowers made him feel sick. He could hear people behind them crying and Aunt Margery, sitting next to him, sobbed. He had never seen so many grown-ups act that way before and it embarrassed him. He stared straight ahead at a big bouquet and tried not to see Aunt Margery getting out her handkerchief and mopping her wet cheeks.

He did not really listen to the Bible readings, but did hear the minister say that Dad had requested that his favourite hymn be read. Jeremy forced himself to listen as the minister began to read.

Be thou my vision, O Lord of my heart . . .

The familiar words soothed him at first but then two lines seemed to jump out at him.

. . . Thou my great Father, I thy true Son,
    Thou in me dwelling, and I with thee one . . .

Jeremy knew it meant God but it sounded as though it were talking about his own father and himself. The bit that went, "I with Thee one," that was how he had felt the night they had seen the owl together.

Then, at last, it was over. His father was being cremated so there was no service at the cemetery. They followed Mum out and Jeremy breathed in a long breath of fresh air. As he stood, half-listening to the murmuring voices of relatives and friends clustering around his mother and aunt, he realized that these hordes of strangers were coming back home with them. He could not understand why and he felt he could not bear it. More standing around and being good and getting kissed! Was it never going to end?

"Uncle Ralph is taking us," Mum told them as they reached the bottom of the steps. "Margery has to drive the Goodwin sisters home."

Uncle Ralph was not really their uncle at all. He was a cousin of Dad's. Mum had said that Jeremy had met him long ago but he didn't remember. He seemed to have nothing in common with Dad.

Not wanting to have to ride home with another stranger, Jeremy gave Sarah a shove to make her get into the car first. Of course, she had to yelp as though he had punched her instead of merely giving her a little push. Uncle Ralph frowned at him and his mother said, "Go easy, Jeremy. . . . That's enough noise, Sarah. Get in and move over."

"I don't want to sit beside him," Sarah protested, her voice rising, cranky and high-pitched.

"Get in," Mum said, "and not one more sound out of either one of you until we get home."

Sarah edged herself across the back seat until she was as far away from him as she could get. Jeremy, seething, got in and slammed the door shut.

"You two kids should know how to behave better than that," Uncle Ralph said heavily as he fitted the key into the ignition. "This is no time to be worrying your mother."

Jeremy was struggling not to cry when Aunt Margery tapped on the window next to him. He rolled it down.

"I was in the drugstore this morning and I got you your heart's desire, Sarah. And some for Jeremy, too."

She handed each of them a small plastic bag. Inside each were licorice twists, red for him and black for Sarah.

"Thanks, Margery," Mum said, her voice breaking. Watching Sarah out of the corner of his eye, Jeremy could see she was trying to tear the end off the plastic bag with her teeth.

"Give it here," he growled at her finally.

She ignored him. Okay for her. Let her sulk like the baby she was.

Then she leaned across the seat and held out the bag. He used his teeth to better effect. When he handed it back to her, opened, she inched closer to him as she took it. He saw that, although she was not crying now, her face was streaked with tears.

Why had she cried when he hadn't? Maybe she had cried when Mum did. It couldn't be because she loved Dad more than he did. How could she?

He bit into his own licorice. Then he turned to her and ordered through a mouthful of candy, "Do up your seatbelt, dummy."

Sarah made a face at him but busied herself looking for the long end of the seatbelt. She found it but could not pull it smoothly enough to get the two ends to meet. He let her struggle with it for a few seconds. Then he leaned across her, adjusted the strap properly and snapped the buckle into place. Sarah looked up and began to laugh.

"We're home, dummy," she said, "and you don't have your own done up."

Uncle Ralph turned and looked at them, his face stern.

"Didn't you hear your mother say you weren't to talk?" he said ponderously, clearly just beginning on a lecture.

Sarah's smile vanished, her body tensed. Jeremy moved fast. He opened the door and slid out in one move.

"She said not to talk till we got home and we are home," he said, knowing he was sounding like a smart-aleck but determined to escape without a scolding from this person he didn't even know. If Mum wanted to bawl him out later, fine. It was none of this guy's business how they behaved.

He spun on his heel and took off, racing to the house. Sarah came panting after him. They left Mum to soothe Uncle Ralph's hurt feelings.

They went straight to Jeremy's room as though they had had it planned ahead of time. Once there, with the door shut tight, the two of them stood and stared at each other.

''Do we have to go out there?'' Sarah asked.

Jeremy, leaning down to stroke Blue, started to shake his head. Then he stopped.

Sarah, who had begun to suck her thumb, something she rarely did now, took it out of her mouth and wiped it on her skirt. He paused, his hand on the doorknob.

She surprised him then by pulling the door open and pushing past him. ''I want Mummy,'' she said and was gone.

So did he. Whether or not she wanted them, he needed her, no matter who else was out there. He shut the door quickly to keep Blue from coming with him and followed his sister.

As he reached the kitchen, he heard Mum laughing. He went on into the living room and was in time to see Sarah march over and lean against her. Mum put her arm around her and smiled over her head at Jeremy.

''These are my two children,'' she said, her pride warm in her voice. ''Jeremy, come and meet one of your father's first students.''

Finally the visitors began to leave. Uncle Ralph, as he was about to go out the front door, astonished Jeremy by slipping a ten-dollar bill into his hand and muttering,

"Get something nice for your mother and sister. You'll know what they'd like. Don't say it's from me."

"But . . ." Jeremy began.

Then he stopped. He knew in that instant that this solemn, awkward man had found the afternoon as long and difficult as he had. He knew, too, that Uncle Ralph had not intended to be mean when he had told them off; he had only been doing his best to help Mum.

"But me no buts," Uncle Ralph said. Then he hurried away.

Only the women who had come to help in the kitchen were left. They were from Mum's church group and she was out there with them.

Jeremy could not stand it inside another minute. He looked around for some excuse to take off. Where was dopey Sarah? As if she had read his mind, she came trotting in with her sweater on and his Frisbee in her hand.

"Mum says we're to go out and get some fresh air," she told him.

As the Frisbee sailed out of his hand and Sarah, across the yard, reached for it and missed, Jeremy felt his life return to normal.

"Sorry," Sarah called, throwing it wild.

"Aim next time," he shouted at her as he went after it.

She laughed as though he had said something really funny. And he felt just the way she sounded. Happy. It seemed years since he had last felt ordinary, everyday happiness. The shadows stretched longer across the grass and it was almost suppertime. Yet the two of them went on playing, paying no attention to the oncoming darkness, until Mum came to the door and called them in.

Twenty

As they entered the house, they found Aunt Margery about to leave. She stood looking at Mum, and her face was worried.

''I know nobody's indispensable, Melly. But I did say I'd chair this meeting and I'm the only one who really knows what it's all about. Yet I hate to leave you . . .''

Mum gave her a quick hug.

''To tell you the truth,'' she said quietly, ''I'd like to be here by myself with only the children for a bit. I don't mean you're like that host of other relatives. You know that. But the three of us do need time together.''

Jeremy followed his mother out to the kitchen. He stood around while she dished up the supper. He couldn't think of anything to say, but that didn't matter. She smiled a welcome and handed him two of the plates.

"Get your hands washed, Sarah," she called. "It's time to eat."

As they took their places, Jeremy felt as though he had been walking a tightrope for days and now he was being allowed to stand on firm ground again. It had been such a polite day. He had had to wear his good clothes. He had even worn a tie. He had been introduced to dozens of total strangers. Then, listening to their talk, he had discovered they were all old friends of Mum's and Dad's. They laughed at things that had happened before he was born and his mother had laughed with them. It had made him feel peculiar. Only now that the crowd had gone and he was back in his jeans, were things coming right again.

"Hey, Sarah, don't hog all the ketchup," he said happily.

Before she could get the bottle righted, a great gush of ketchup drowned the noodles on her plate. She glared at him.

"You made me do that," she accused. "Why don't you mind your own business?"

Grinning at her, he reached across and exchanged his plate with hers.

"There," he said amicably, "I like lots of ketchup. Now you can try again. Or do you want me to do it for you, sissy."

"*No!*" she roared at him. Then, eyeing the bottle, she added, "Mum can do it."

Both he and Mum laughed and, after struggling not to, Sarah gave in and joined them. All at once Jeremy felt hungry, really hungry, for the first time that day. He began to eat ravenously.

"Although I find your nobility truly inspiring, Jeremy," his mother said, "I still wish that you would take smaller mouthfuls. We are not having a race; we are having a meal."

Sarah giggled. He didn't mind. When Mum started nagging him about his table manners, life was back to normal. With a flourish of his fork, he took one pea off his plate and managed to make it into three minute bites. Sarah was convulsed by this. Mum gave him a pained look.

Ten minutes later, their happy mood was shattered. It happened so suddenly that Jeremy was caught completely off guard. Mum had started serving dessert when Sarah looked up, as if she had just remembered something, and asked, "Where has Daddy gone?"

Jeremy went rigid. He wanted to hit her, hit her hard. He wanted to slap that dopey look off her stupid face. It was as if Sarah had betrayed them.

Mum's hand closed on his wrist. He had not realized that he was getting to his feet until she drew him back down onto his chair. Her grasp was not ungentle but the strength in it left him startled and still.

Then she spoke in a voice as strong and as steady as her hold had been.

"Daddy's dead, Sarah. I thought you understood that."

The little girl stared at her mother.

"When you sent me to take Mrs. Barr's dish back, Rodney was there and he said he was sorry Daddy had died but Mrs. Barr told him not to say that. She said that Daddy was just away on a trip."

As she told them this, her eyes had grown wide and her words, confident at first, began to falter. Mum sighed and then took a deep breath.

"This time Rodney was right, honey. Daddy did die. I suppose Mrs. Barr thought you were too little to understand, that's all. She was trying to make things easier for you."

Sarah looked indignant.

"I'm *not* too little," she started to protest automatically. Then, without warning, she burst into tears.

Mum stood up, went swiftly to Sarah and gathered the weeping child into her arms. She settled down with her in the big, high-backed rocker where she had taken them whenever they needed comforting, for as far back as he could remember. She rocked Sarah back and forth and murmured soft, hushing sounds until her sobs quieted. Then she began to sing to her.

Hush, little Sarah, don't say a word.
Mama's going to buy you a mockingbird.
If that mockingbird don't sing,
Mama's going to buy you a diamond ring.
If that diamond ring turns brass,
Mama's going to buy you a looking glass . . .

Dad was dead. The hurt of this squeezed Jeremy like a giant hand. All the blessed familiarity of tossing the Frisbee back and forth and laughing together at the start of supper was torn from him.

He was too big, he knew, to be rocked, too big to cry the way Sarah was crying. He had to do something, though. Battling a feeling that this was a betrayal greater than Sarah's, he picked up his spoon and began to eat his dessert. It was johnnycake with maple syrup. One of the church ladies had brought it. It was good, too, sweet and hot and crunchy on the outside, exactly the way he liked it. By the time he had finished scraping the dish for the last drop of syrup, Sarah had recovered and was ready to come and have hers. Her face was crumpled and flushed.

"Ready for some more, Jeremy?" Mum asked.

She began to cut him another helping without waiting for his reply. He usually wanted three. But he shook his head without looking at her. Inside his head he was hearing the words of that song, over and over and over again. "Mama's going to buy you . . ." it kept repeating. A diamond ring. A looking glass. A horse and cart . . . Mama's going to buy you . . . Mama's going to buy you . . .

That was how it was going to be from now on. Never again would Dad buy them anything. Never again would he hand out their allowances or give them the money to buy a popsicle or a comic book. Never again.

"May I please be excused?" His words sounded out, loud and abrupt. Without waiting for her reply, he shoved his chair back and bolted.

He went straight to his own room and closed the door behind him. Then he went to his desk and sat down and opened his math text. He found the page he had been assigned for homework on the day Dad had died. As he scanned it, searching for where to begin, the print blurred before his eyes. He blinked hard. The words and figures were clear again. You'd have to be nuts to cry over math unless you were as big a bawl-baby as Sarah. He picked up his pencil and got to work.

He had never liked math all that much, but tonight the numbers soothed him. Each time he finished a problem and checked his answer he felt stronger. The neatness of it, the exactness of it, drew him back to safety and away from the storm of anger and grief that had almost swept his self-control away during supper.

It was nearly eight-thirty when Mum knocked at his door. He had been waiting for that light tap, had counted on her coming, but he did not want to talk. He had nothing to say.

"Come in." He stayed bent over his book but he heard her open the door.

"I've got a lot of homework to do," he muttered, without putting down his pencil or taking his eyes off Problem 12. He did not tell her that he was already four pages ahead of where he thought the class would be by now. He stared down at the neat columns of figures, trying to concentrate.

"Well, don't stay up too late," she said after a moment. "I'm going to start getting ready for bed myself. It's been a long day."

She hesitated then for a moment, giving him time to speak. When he did not, she went on quickly, "If you want me for anything, come and find me. Wake me up if you want to. Goodnight, son."

Why did she have to call him "son"? Why didn't she just leave?

"Goodnight," he said, turning a little but not far enough so that he could really see her.

Deep inside him, a voice was crying out to her to come in, to make the pain in him stop. But he could not tell her. He was not even letting himself hear it. He willed her to go.

"Take care of him for me, Blue," she said softly. Then she left. She closed the door behind her. When he heard it click shut, Jeremy did turn. Then he jerked back around on his chair, swallowed hard and began on Problem 13.

Twenty-one

The morning after the funeral, the three Talbots left Blue with Mrs. Barr and went to the cottage. It was cold but sunny and the trees were ablaze with autumn colour. They read, went for hikes and picnics despite the nip in the wind. Mum spent a lot of time sitting looking out over the lake.

They all missed Dad but they had been there without him before. It felt more as if he were coming to join them soon than as if he would never be with them again.

One evening, Sarah, in a subdued voice, asked Mum what heaven was like. Their mother sat quietly for a moment. Neither Jeremy nor Sarah spoke. Then Melly Talbot said slowly, "I don't know, Sarah. Nobody really knows."

"But is Daddy an . . . an angel?"

Jeremy wished she would shut up. But while he was

trying to come up with a way to squelch her, Mum went on.

"Think of some of the wonderful surprises there are in this world. Think of a caterpillar turning into a butterfly. Think of a brown seed growing into a flower. If God has arranged things like that for a caterpillar and a seed, I trust him to know what to do with us. But the picture we have of heaven as a place with golden streets and pearly gates, where angels play on harps and God sits on a big throne, comes from a book in the Bible called Revelations."

She paused for a moment.

"I think the writer was trying to say that heaven must be more beautiful than anything we can imagine. I don't think he meant us to believe it was really the way he said it was. But there is one part in that book that I love. It was read at the funeral but you probably didn't take it in. Let me find it and read it to you."

She fetched her Bible and found the place. Jeremy liked listening to her read the Bible. She used her own voice, not a special Bible-reading voice like the minister's. As she read the words, he did remember hearing them before.

Then I saw a new Heaven and a new earth, for the first Heaven and the first earth had disappeared and the sea was no more. I saw the holy city, the new Jerusalem, descending from God out of Heaven, prepared as a bride dressed in beauty for her husband. Then I heard a great voice from the throne crying, "See! The home of God is with men and he will live among them. They shall be his people and God himself shall be with them, and will wipe away every tear from their eyes. Death shall be no more and never again shall there be sorrow or crying or pain. For all these former things are passed and gone.''

When she stopped reading, neither of them said anything. She closed the book and took it back into her bedroom. When she came out again, Jeremy could see she had been crying. But she said, ''Put on some music, Jeremy. I'm going to get marshmallows for us to toast when the fire dies down a little.''

Sarah wasn't content to let him choose, of course, and loudly demanded *There's a Hippo in My Bathtub*. Jeremy groaned, but really he thought it was a lot better than most of her other favourites. He did not remember what songs were on the record until Anne Murray began to sing the familiar words.

Hush, little baby, don't say a word.
Papa's going to buy you a mockingbird . . .

Papa. Why did she say ''papa''? Jeremy stiffened and forgot to keep his marshmallows a safe distance from the last small tongue of fire. By the time he'd blown out the flame and eaten the blackened candy, declaring that he'd burned it on purpose because he liked it that way, the song had ended. He saw his mother looking at him. She knew he was lying. Maybe she even knew why. He jumped up, banging into the table as he did so, and snatched the bag of marshmallows from Sarah.

''Don't be such a pig,'' he told her roughly. ''Men get served before girls.''

''There aren't any *men* here,'' Sarah yelled, grabbing it back.

Mum made no comment. When the two of them were

back in front of the fire again, she got up and put the rest of the marshmallows away. Still ignoring their sulky silence, she returned and said, ''It's late, but how about a game of Monopoly before we go to bed? You'll have to suspend hostilities, of course, but I have a feeling none of us is ready to go to sleep yet.''

Jeremy's anger was gone as suddenly as it had come. He saw a smile light up Sarah's face. He eased his perfectly toasted marshmallows off the fork, popped them both into his mouth and said, speaking indistinctly, ''Okay. You be banker. You're the oldest.''

Memory touched him with sadness again but his sister sent it packing.

''How come I never get to be oldest?''

As the other two laughed, she hastily revised her question.

''I mean, how come I never get to be banker?''

''Arithmetic plays a part in it, sweetheart,'' Mum told her, ''but this time you do get to be banker's assistant.''

Sarah stopped pouting. Jeremy fetched the box from the pile of games. Mum won as usual. Although he said it wasn't fair, Jeremy found that he was secretly more glad than sorry. It was reassuring to know that some things didn't change.

Though their days at the cottage were good days, he was glad when Monday morning came and it was time to go back to school. He did not ride his bike but walked with Sarah the way he had done the day Dad went to the hospital. When they were halfway there, she began to skip along at his side.

''Miss Goldberg doesn't know that Daddy died.'' She was clearly looking forward to breaking the news and being the centre of attention.

"She probably read it in the paper," he said curtly.

Sarah's jaunty step slowed but only for a moment.

"The kids in my class don't read the paper."

Why spoil it for her? In spite of her questions about heaven and the way she had burst into tears at supper-time after the funeral, he could tell she didn't understand yet, not really.

"Come on or we'll be late," he urged, quickening his own pace.

Once inside the school, he paid no attention to kids who stared and whispered or to others who turned away as if the sight of him upset them. He knew how they felt. He remembered when Maria White's mother had been in a car crash. She hadn't been killed but she had been badly injured and he had hated seeing Maria. Each time he had caught a glimpse of her pale, anxious face, he'd wanted to get away from her fast. If her mother could be hurt and maybe never walk again, anybody's mother could. Thinking of this helped him to understand how the other kids must feel about him now, but their averted glances and lowered voices still hurt him. They turned him into an outsider.

He was marching along, eyes front, chin high, when a hand touched his elbow. Startled, he turned and saw Tess Medford.

"I was scared I was going to be late," she burst out in a rush. "The students upstairs found a lost puppy last night and they let me see him this morning. Is he ever cute! I hope they'll keep him. I asked Grandpa if they could and he says there's nothing in the lease about no pets but he isn't happy about it . . . Did you hear about the play?"

Jeremy shook his head.

"On Friday there were auditions for a play," she rushed on. "Kim tried out for a part. So did Michael Esch and Katy, I think. I don't know if they got the parts, though."

She looked away from him suddenly and then, just as suddenly, faced him again.

"I'm sorry about your father. He was the best teacher I ever had."

When she saw he was at a loss for words, she went on talking. "Has Blue been exploring again?"

"No," he answered. "Not yet."

He wished he knew how to thank her. She hadn't avoided him and she hadn't looked at him as if he were a stranger, not even when she had been speaking about Dad. Maybe she knew how much it mattered to him. After all, she must feel like an outsider most of the time.

They had moved toward the classroom as they talked, but before they actually got there Tess turned away, mumbling that she needed to get something from her locker. He looked after her, hesitated and then went on alone.

As she came through the door a few seconds later, she glanced over at him. Then she pretended she hadn't.

She couldn't guess, could she, that he didn't want the others to see him walking with her? He had an uncomfortable feeling that she didn't just guess; she knew.

When Jeremy was eating his lunch, it dawned on him that he and Sarah had not needed to take their lunches today. Why hadn't Mum mentioned it? They were so in the habit now that he had done it automatically.

He glanced across at where Tess was sitting a little apart from the other girls. She was reading. When he had finished, he walked past her and glanced at the spine of the book. He stopped short and his mouth opened with surprise. It was a library copy of *Kim*. She appeared to be nearly at the end.

"Where did you hear about that book?" he demanded.

Her glance flew up to his face and then down to the page in front of her again. A flush stained her cheeks.

"You were reading it and you seemed so interested . . . I thought I'd try it," she muttered. Then her shoulders straightened and her chin lifted. "Anyway, there's no law against reading whatever I like," she flashed, flipping her long braid over her shoulder with a defiant toss. Yet, fierce as her words were, she kept her voice low. The others could not hear. Remembering belatedly where he was, he lowered his.

"When you're done, I'd like to talk to you about it," he found himself saying. He hesitated. "Dad told me to read it."

The light of battle left her eyes.

"I only have one chapter left to go. I hope it has a happy ending but don't tell me."

He felt sorry for her. Although she might not find the ending as disappointing as he had.

"That's what I want to talk about," he said, teasing her with the fact that he knew and she didn't.

She laughed, a silent laugh he alone knew about. She was being careful even though by this time half the class had seen that they were talking together.

"Go away and let me read it then," she growled, her eyes bright.

"I think you'd like her," his dad had said. He'd been right, Jeremy admitted to himself. But making friends with her, real friends, was something else again. The rest of the kids could make it tough for him if they found out. Just the same, he decided to risk talking to her a minute longer. By now everybody had seen them, anyway.

''If you get it finished this afternoon, we could walk home together part way,'' he murmured.

''I'll get it finished,'' she said, bending her head over the book again.

As he went swiftly out of the lunchroom, he felt shaken. Still it wasn't as if he'd promised to walk home with her every day. She wouldn't be dumb enough to wait for him on the front steps of the school, would she? What if she called out to him . . . ?

He caught himself stewing and with an effort, managed to stop. He'd just have to trust in her good sense. If he'd made a mistake, he could live it down.

Twenty-two

When Jeremy came out of school, Tess was nowhere in sight. He said goodbye to the other boys and set out for home. He did not loiter or look for her. She'd show up when she was ready.

As he turned the corner, leaving the school building three blocks behind, he saw her. She was leaning up against the trunk of a tree, staring off into the distance as though she was not expecting a soul. His pace quickened.

"Hi," he said off-handedly when he was near enough.

"Hi," she answered and fell into step beside him.

Her casual tone made it clear that he was not doing her any great favour by meeting her. He liked that.

"Did you finish the book?"

She nodded.

"How did you like it?"

She took her time replying. He waited.

"I liked parts of it a lot," she said slowly. "I liked his

learning about the jewels and the part when he found out who he was. All the different people were great and the adventures. It was awfully long, though, and there were boring parts. I didn't like the ending one bit.''

''Me, neither!'' Jeremy was delighted. ''I wanted them to find something really great and then it just petered out.''

''Yeah,'' Tess frowned. ''We must have missed something, I guess. After all, your dad told you to read it and it's a classic. It must be good, really. Maybe we're too young . . .'' She sounded unconvinced.

''Well, I'll read it again when I'm thirty-five and decide,'' Jeremy said.

Tess laughed. Neither of them really believed they would ever be thirty-five.

When Jeremy arrived home, Blue was waiting. She appeared annoyed but he wasn't all that late. He dumped his books on the hall table and bent to stroke her. But before he could begin to play with her properly, Mum was there.

''Jeremy, I went shopping but stupidly forgot to get more milk. Would you please run over to the store and pick up a bag? Here's the money.''

Jeremy did not want to go to the store for milk. He was not in the mood.

''Can't Sarah go?'' he asked, his attention still on Blue.

''Your sister is helping me get supper or I'm sure she would be only too pleased to go,'' Mum said coolly. ''You are the person in this family who downs two glasses of milk at every meal and a few more in between. You'd think you were a calf!''

Jeremy didn't laugh. He was well aware that she was tired and that she just wanted him to take the money and go willingly. But all of a sudden he felt as though he had been being good forever. He hadn't had any milk yet and he always had a glass when he came in from school. Had she thought of that? He was still standing there feeling grouchy when she added bitingly, "Jeremy, I have a great deal to get done before we eat. I'm counting on you to do your share."

Suddenly he knew that was the whole trouble. He did not want to be counted on. Knowing he was on dangerous ground, he muttered, "I just don't feel like it, that's all."

"It's too bad about how you feel, young man. Get going and be back here in less than half an hour. Move!"

He had made her mad, good and mad. He could tell by the way she thrust the change purse into his hand, by the way she shoved him through the front door and by the way she slammed the door hard behind him. As he climbed on his bike, Jeremy felt more cheerful. She was her old self.

Kim Chiong, also doing an errand, was in the store. The two boys came out together.

"Give me a ride as far as your place?" he asked.

Jeremy knew he wasn't supposed to. Dad had absolutely forbidden riding two on a bike. But it wasn't all that dangerous. If he'd been downtown now, that would be different. But there would be hardly any cars on the route from the corner store to his own house. Who could it hurt?

"Okay. Hop on."

Kim perched on the crossbar and they were off. Then, as bad luck would have it, just as Jeremy was slowing down to let Kim jump off, his mother stepped out the front door to get the evening paper.

She waited until Kim had gone before she lit into him. She finished off by saying, "I'm disappointed in you, Jeremy." Then she sent him to his room.

He flung himself down on his bed, hating everybody he knew. Even Blue had deserted him. He opened the door a crack. No cat waited there. As he eased it shut again, though, he heard the sound of muffled sobbing from Sarah's room. So she was in trouble, too!

Jeremy leaned against the door, standing with his ear pressed against it. Then he heard his mother's voice, exasperated, tired, but with a trace of wry laughter in it.

"Blue," she was saying, "I'm a failure. I've raised two monsters, miserable little wretches."

Jeremy could hear Blue make a sound in answer. He grinned. He could picture her, sitting very straight and alert, her eyes never leaving Mum's face.

"What a good suggestion! Leave them on somebody's doorstep," his mother said. "But, Blue, I can't, not at this late date. I taught them their names and address."

At that, Jeremy Talbot opened his door and went to join her. Never before had he come out of his room when he had been sent there as a punishment, until one of his parents had come to release him. But that didn't seem important now. What if she did count on him? That wasn't so terrible. He counted on her, didn't he?

"Hey, lady, lovely lady," he said, doing his best to imitate an Italian chef he had seen on TV, "I make-a da grand pizza. You sit on de chair and . . . and . . ."

" . . . and sew a fine seam," Mum finished for him. "And feed upon strawberries, sugar and cream. Not on your life. Not after that wonderful offer of assistance."

When the three of them sat down to eat, Mum looked at them with a funny smile. "You two think you've been busy today while I've been loafing around. But wait till I tell you what I've really done.''

They waited, forks suspended, expecting a long list of errands or some tremendous housekeeping feat. They were totally unprepared when she announced, ''I've applied to go back to school full time and I've been accepted. I start this Wednesday.''

''School!'' Sarah echoed. ''You're too old to go to school.''

As far back as Jeremy could remember, Mum had been attending lectures, mostly at night. She wanted to work with kids like Gilly Hopkins, kids who didn't have good homes. But why was she making a big deal about something that she'd been doing all along? He looked at her, his expression polite but puzzled.

''Full time, Jeremy! I think you missed the important word. I'll be going every day, all day long, the way you do. If I work extremely hard, I can get my degree in one year. But I'll only be able to do it if you two help.''

''Help how?'' Sarah asked.

''You're not going to like this.'' Mum spoke firmly but with sympathy, too. ''You can help by putting your dirty clothes in the wash instead of under the bed, by making those same beds before you leave for school, by setting the table without fussing about whose turn it is, by hanging your towels up, by doing all kinds of small, essential jobs that will make life possible.''

Sarah looked downright mutinous. Jeremy knew exactly how she felt. He glanced at Mum. He knew, by the determined set of her jaw, that there was no hope of making her change her mind. They were in for a hard winter.

''That's not all,'' Melly Talbot said then. ''We might as well get all the shocks over at once. I'm putting this house up for sale.''

Jeremy was flabbergasted. This time, questions poured out of him.

''Why? You mean soon? Where would we live? What's wrong with here?''

''You sound like Margery,'' his mother said. ''She thinks I'm out of my mind. But your father and I discussed it when we knew he wasn't . . . coming back. Without his salary, I can't swing the mortgage payments. If we sold the cottage, we might manage to keep it, but . . .''

''Sell the cottage!'' they cried, horrified.

''I was sure you'd feel that way. I think we'll move into an apartment for the present.''

''An apartment!'' Sarah said, excitement in her voice now. ''Like Mercy Phillpot's?''

Her mother laughed.

''No, not quite like Mercy's. We don't need a place with a doorman and a sauna and maid service and palatial rooms. The rent would be far beyond what we can afford. At any rate, I've certainly given myself plenty to keep me occupied in the next few months. That alone makes it a good idea, as far as I'm concerned.''

Jeremy knew what she meant. He'd been glad to return to school this morning because he didn't want to have nothing to do but sit and think. He had felt guilty about this need to keep busy, but if she felt that way, too, it must be okay.

''What will we do with Blue?'' Sarah's eyes were suddenly tragic. ''They don't allow pets in apartments. Mercy can't even have a bird!''

"Some apartments take pets," Mum assured her. "I'll just have to hunt until I find one. I don't think Jeremy would come with us if it meant leaving his cat behind."

"They take animals at Tess Medford's place," Jeremy said suddenly. "It's a house made over into three apartments. It's on Maplewood. If we lived there, we wouldn't have to change schools . . . only they probably don't have an apartment vacant."

He felt deflated all at once. For one second, it had seemed such a great idea. Yet would he want to live in the same house as Tess Medford? He sat thinking about it while Sarah cleared away the plates and Mum served the dessert.

I wouldn't mind, he thought in surprise. I wouldn't mind at all.

The next afternoon when Jeremy set out for home, the wind buffeted him with a totally unexpected wallop. A drift of fallen leaves swirled up around his knees and others came flying down from the trees. His hair blew into his eyes and, when he twisted his head to avoid the gale, it blew straight up on end. He laughed aloud. Nobody would want to stay inside on a wonderful, wild day like this.

He turned the first corner and began to run, the wind pushing at him. His arms were bent as he started and, momentarily, he stretched them out wide, feeling as if at any minute he might be tossed up into the sky and start to soar like a bird.

Suddenly Tess was running at his side, her long skirt flapping, her face exultant, her braid streaming out behind her.

"Isn't it great?" he yelled.

"Magnificent!" she shouted back.

"Superb!"

It took her a split second to come up with another word but only a split second.

"Tremendous and stupendous!" she bellowed.

As she did so, the wind dropped for an instant and her voice sounded out loudly in the hush. They both laughed crazily, though she did look a bit abashed. Running out of breath simultaneously, they slowed to a walk.

Then the rain came. It arrived with a rush, spattering their faces. It grew heavier in a matter of seconds. They would have been drenched to the skin if Tess hadn't spotted shelter in the doorway of a nearby church. She grabbed Jeremy's arm and gestured toward it with a jerk of her head.

They both leaned up against the huge old doors, breath-less and speechless. Then the rain came driving in at them in a wet, wild gust. Jeremy, certain the church would be locked, nevertheless turned and tried the door. The next instant it was swinging wide and letting them dash into a shadowy vestibule. They stood there staring at each other uncertainly.

"Do you think it's all right to stay here?" he asked in a whisper.

Tess shrugged. "It's an Anglican church. Are you an Anglican?"

"No. We're United. Are you?"

"Well, Grandma was Baptist so we went there when she was alive. Now we mostly go to the United, too."

"The rain ought to be over soon. It sure blew up fast enough. We might as well stay in here till it stops." Tess had ventured halfway up the stairs, exploring. She looked extra tall and ghostly in the dim light.

''We can watch for it to stop through this little window,''
she called softly.

She seated herself on the step next to it. Jeremy
hesitated. Should they really go that far away from the
door? What if somebody popped out from somewhere
and caught them?

''Chicken!'' Tess said.

Unable to think of a smart answer, Jeremy climbed up
and sat down beside her. Suddenly he remembered he
had a lot to tell her.

''Wait till you hear the news. We're going to move into
an apartment. We have to find one that'll take cats. I told
Mum about the puppy at your place and I think she's
going to see your grandfather. You don't have an empty
apartment, do you?''

Tess's face lit up. Then she looked not quite so sure.

''Those boys never came home last night,'' she told
him. ''When the puppy kept crying, Grandpa used his
key. They were behind in their rent. All their stuff was
gone. Boy, is it ever a mess in there! They let the puppy
go wherever he wanted and they stuck stuff all over the
walls and spilled something behind the stove. Grandpa
says it will have to be cleaned and redecorated. He took
the puppy to the humane society this morning. The apartment is vacant, all right, but whoever moves in will have
to wait till it's fixed up.''

She stopped talking and a silence fell. Jeremy was sure
Mum wouldn't mind putting off moving. Tess liked the
idea of his family going to live there, didn't she? Maybe
he shouldn't have said anything until Mum had talked
to Mr. Medford.

Then Tess reached out and touched his arm. He looked
around and she pulled her hand back quickly.

"You asked me once if my parents died." She was speaking in such a low voice that he could hardly hear her. He waited, keeping his face blank.

"I didn't want to talk about it so I snapped at you," she said. "But now . . . now we're sort of friends . . ."

Her voice died away. She was not looking at him.

"It's okay," he said. "I shouldn't have asked you."

"You weren't being nosy. And I want to tell you now. Well, maybe I don't want to tell you but I want you to know. It's just that it's hard for me to talk about Gwen."

Jeremy was bewildered. Who on earth was Gwen? Before he could stop himself, the words popped out.

"Who's Gwen?" he asked her.

Tess took a deep breath. She seemed to be bracing herself, too.

"Gwen is my mother," she said.

Twenty-three

Jeremy could feel his cheeks reddening. He was glad the light in the church was dim. He tried to keep the curiosity out of his voice.

"You don't have to tell me anything," he said.

"I know I don't have to but I'm going to." Tess sounded angry. "Now shut up and listen."

Jeremy sat, holding his breath.

"My mother was only sixteen when she had me," Tess's words burst out. "She wasn't married and she didn't want me. Nobody wanted me. She wouldn't say who my father was."

She paused long enough to draw in breath. Jeremy kept quiet.

"When she knew I was coming, she decided to give me up for adoption," Tess went on. "I don't know what happened exactly. Grandpa still puts me off if I ask questions. Lots of times, when he doesn't know what to say, he won't answer at all. Gwen left when I was just a kid. Grandma was the one who made Gwen keep me. She felt responsible for me, even though I was a burden.''

Tess gave herself a little shake, shot him a glance and picked up the story once more.

''Grandpa, Grandma and Gwen and I moved away from Riverside right after I was born.''

''Where did you go?'' Jeremy asked.

''To Toronto,'' Tess answered. ''Grandma wouldn't tell anybody here our new address. She wanted to make a fresh start.''

Jeremy had a dozen questions to ask but he made himself wait. At last, doing his best to keep his voice casual, he asked the one question that seemed safe.

''Did you call her Gwen?''

Tess's mouth twisted in what might have been a smile.

''She made me call her Gwen. She didn't want a kid my size tagging around calling her Mum. When I started kindergarten, I was as big as some of the kids in grade two. Gwen hated my being a giant.''

Tess was flinging her story at him as if daring him to pity her. He thought of her, head and shoulders above the other girls in kindergarten. Had her clothes been old-fashioned then, too? Imagine having to call your mother by her first name!

''She was really pretty, though, Gwen,'' Tess said softly. ''I don't take after her. She had pale blonde hair. I guess she bleached it but I thought it was beautiful. Sometimes she let me comb it. I thought she looked like a fairy princess. I know now that she didn't love me but I loved her. That's why I couldn't believe it when she went away

and left me behind. Like a dope, I kept waiting for her to
come back. Sometimes even now I get to thinking she
still might. . . . She went away on New Year's Eve, the
day before my seventh birthday.''

Jeremy turned to stare at her.

''Is your birthday on New Year's?'' he demanded. Tess
scowled.

''It's just that mine is on December 31st,'' he explained
hastily. ''We must be almost twins.''

Tess's face relaxed.

''Not identical twins, though,'' she said.

He looked at her long legs, stretched out in front of
them, and reaching down a full step beyond his. But
now he wished he hadn't distracted her.

''Where did . . .did your mother go?'' he asked. He
couldn't bring himself to call her Gwen.

''How should I know?'' Tess snapped, glaring.

Before he could stammer an apology, she realized he
had meant no harm. She beat him to it.

''I'm sorry. It's just that she never wrote, not even a
card. She was going out with a man Grandma hated. I
hated him, too. He called me the brat. Grandma found
out later that he was already married and that he ended
up going back to his wife. So wherever Gwen is now,
she's not with him. But she never wrote. She never even
phoned. Not once in nearly five years.''

''You mean you don't know where your own mother
is?'' Jeremy couldn't believe it.

''You've got it. I don't know and I don't care.'' Tess's
words now sounded hard and sharp like thrown stones.
''She's not interested in me so why should I care about
her? I try to forget her. That's the easiest way. I used to

moon over her picture but I quit. She's gone for good and I'm glad.''

Jeremy shifted his position, edging away from her. Her mouth had clamped shut and her eyes were hard and defiant. He looked away.

Forgetting *was* the easiest way. When he forgot Dad was dead, when he forgot Dad altogether and concentrated on other things, then life was easier. When something made him think of his father — birds flying south, a song the two of them had liked coming over the radio, the sight of Dad's name written in the front of a book — he felt so mixed-up, lonely and scared that he wished with all his heart that he had not been made to remember.

If Tess needed to forget, too, it couldn't be wrong. It was as though he had been walking all alone down a long dark road and now, unexpectedly, someone had come to walk beside him.

Tess brought him out of his private thoughts with a jolt.

''Well, does all this matter to you or doesn't it?'' she demanded fiercely, her eyes drilling holes into him. ''Will your mother still want to move into the apartment when she hears?''

Jeremy gaped at her. How had his mother come into this? He pulled himself together.

''Are you nuts? None of it's your fault. And what does it have to do with my mother, for Pete's sake?''

Tess looked abashed for an instant. Her glance left his face and went to her hands, now knotted in her lap. ''After Gwen left, Grandma told me never to talk about her, or anything that had happened at home. She made me come straight home from school and I couldn't have kids over to play. Not that there were loads of them begging to come!''

"You must have had some friends," Jeremy said, hoping it was true.

Tess's voice was flat.

"You know how kids ask you questions. Hardly anything was safe to say. So I stopped talking. What was the point of trying to make friends? I was so much bigger, too . . . and there were my clothes."

He caught his breath but said nothing.

"Grandma made them herself. She didn't approve of what the other girls wore."

"But she's not making your clothes now and they still . . . " Jeremy stopped short, his face burning. Why couldn't he keep his big mouth shut?

But Tess didn't get mad. She just went on looking at her hands. And the words, aching with long shame, kept coming.

"I hate shopping for clothes. It might be okay if I had someone to go with but I don't. So when I have to get something, I go to the Dollar Dresses. The only things long enough are women's dresses and they're the wrong shape. I can mend and sew on buttons but I can't make a dress over properly. Grandpa never notices. He doesn't care what I wear as long as I don't wear pants. So I do know how weird I look but I can't help it."

She sounded so miserable that Jeremy felt she shouldn't be telling him these private things. But something in the way she came out with the whole story made him know she had been needing someone to talk to for a long time. He thought of the afternoon he had gone looking for her because he had had to tell somebody that his father was dying.

Suddenly Tess jumped up and went down the stairs at a run, leaving him staring after her. A moment later she was pulling open the big front door of the church. Past her, Jeremy could see the rain still driving down. Without a backward glance at him, she plunged out into it and disappeared.

"Hey!" Jeremy yelled.

He sprang up and followed. Leaning far out into the downpour, he could see her racing up the street.

"Tess, wait!"

She did not slacken her pace. There was no way he could catch up with her, either, giraffe that she was, if she didn't want to be caught. He stood there, hoping the rain would let up but it fell steadily. Well, his skin was waterproof even if his clothes weren't. Following Tess's example, he set out for home.

As he splashed along, he thought of how Tess had said she used to love her mother. It was hard to imagine having a mother like that but of course you would love her, no matter what. Kids had to love their mothers. He didn't know why but he was sure it was true. If his mother had gone away when he was only just turning seven and had never written him even one postcard, would he still love her? He could not imagine it, however hard he tried.

Twenty-four

When Jeremy squelched in through the front door, he found Mum talking on the phone. He gave her a wave and stooped to greet Blue. Blue backed away from his wet hand.

"Okay for you, puss," he said, straightening. Then he heard what his mother was saying.

"Can we come to see the apartment tonight?"

Jeremy went and stood beside her, not even pretending not to eavesdrop. She smiled at him and went on listening.

"Wonderful," she said a moment later. "We'll be there around eight, then."

The instant she hung up, he pounced.

"Who was that? Was it Tess's grandfather? What did he say? Are we going to rent their apartment?"

She laughed at him.

"One question at a time, if you please. Go and remove

those sopping clothes and I'll come along and tell you all I know, which isn't much.''

She pushed him ahead of her but he walked backwards so they could continue talking without his missing a word.

''That *was* Mr. Medford,'' she said. ''They *do* have a vacancy but apparently . . .''

''I know about the mess it's in,'' he interrupted. ''But if we like it, when would we move?''

''Mr. Medford says it won't be ready for new tenants till at least the end of October. But we won't be ready to move anywhere until then, anyway.''

Jeremy was stripping off his wet socks as he took this in. He stopped suddenly, with the second one only half off, and blurted, ''Do you know about Tess, Mum?''

''Know what about her?'' she asked, reaching to tweak the sock free.

''Know about her not having a father and about her mother going away and leaving her?''

''Yes, Jeremy, I've known that for some time. I guess things have been rough for Tess. Did she tell you about her mother?''

Jeremy nodded.

''She doesn't know where her mother is,'' he burst out.

Mum sat down in his armchair and looked at him for a long moment. Then she spoke.

''I wasn't going to tell you just yet but perhaps this is the time,'' she said slowly. ''Tess's birthday, Jeremy, is on January 1st.''

''I know,'' he said, puzzled. ''It's the day after mine. She told me.''

''What neither of you knows is that Gwen Medford

and I shared the same hospital room. You were born in the afternoon and Tess arrived just after midnight. She was twice your size, I remember, and she had lots of hair while you were bald as an egg.''

His eyes widened.

''You mean you saw Tess when she was just born? How come you never told me?''

''We never really talked about her till today, did we?'' she answered. ''And it didn't concern you. It still doesn't, but you will hear me talking to Mr. Medford tonight like an old friend. I'd rather you understood now. He used to chat with me sometimes when his wife was fussing over Gwen.''

''What was she . . . Gwen . . . like?'' he demanded.

''She was very young, not old enough to have a child.''

''Tess says nobody wanted her. That's crazy, isn't it? None of it is Tess's fault.''

''If Tess thinks she was unwanted, she's wrong,'' Melly Talbot said. ''They didn't have to keep her, Jeremy. What matters is that Tess has not had an easy time of it. Gwen was so young. She couldn't have been a very satisfactory mother. I think her parents gave her everything she wanted when she was little and then had no idea what to do with her when she became a teenager. She was lovely to look at but she wasn't happy. Tess should try to understand and forgive her.''

Jeremy was not touched by this. Whether Gwen was pretty or unhappy had nothing to do with it. She had no business being mean to Tess. She was her mother, for crying out loud!

''She never wrote Tess a letter, not even a postcard,'' he said, his voice hard as steel. ''And she hasn't phoned, either, not once.''

His mother sighed.

"Her grandfather told your father that they didn't hear from her but I didn't realize they had never heard at all. It's a sad story. I'm glad you've become Tess's friend."

He didn't deny it. As she said the words, he felt a glow of satisfaction. It was as if Dad knew now that he had actually done the thing Dad had asked of him. He had not been too young, after all.

The front door banged. His mother stood up, stooping to collect his wet clothes.

"That'll be your sister." Then she took another look at him and frowned.

"I'm sure that underwear is wet, too," she said. "Take it off and put on something dry."

"Okay, okay," he said, making no move to obey. He was not about to strip stark naked with her standing watching, even if she was his mother.

She got the message. With a little smile that maddened him, she made for the door. She thought he was cute! And there wasn't a thing he could do about it.

When she was gone, shutting the door behind her, he grabbed dry things out of his chest of drawers, went over to where his closet door hid him and skinned out of his underpants. He was all dressed again in a matter of seconds. Sarah had been taught to knock on a closed door, but she didn't always remember. Neither did Mum if it came to that. Living in a house full of women wasn't easy.

Jeremy flopped down on his bed and began to think over everything he'd learned that afternoon. Two hours ago he'd never heard of Gwen. Wait until he told Tess that Mum had seen her the very day she was born. He would not pass on the bit about him being bald.

Dad would be pleased with him, he thought. He had said he couldn't make friends with Tess but he'd been wrong. He knew she really must like him or she'd never have told him all that stuff about her family. He smiled.

Then, from somewhere deep in his memory, one sentence sounded.

"If you make friends with her, the others would soon follow."

He shifted uneasily. He'd *made* friends with her! It wasn't his fault she never spoke to him in school. He'd answer if she did. She didn't want the other kids to know they were friends any more than he did. They'd never hear the end of it. Jeremy was doing her a favour by not drawing attention to their friendship. If his father were here, he could explain. Dad would see that he was right.

Twenty-five

*T*he Talbots arrived on the Medfords' doorstep at two minutes past eight. Mr. Medford opened the door.

"Hello, Mrs. Talbot," he said. "Come in." Jeremy looked up and saw a tall, white-haired man with a craggy face and jutting eyebrows. He sounded gruff. Sarah drew back a little.

Although Mr. Medford owned the whole house, he and Tess lived in the basement apartment. They all followed him down some stairs, turned left at the foot and saw before them an open door leading into what clearly was a living room. Tess stood up as they appeared. She looked taller than usual and self-conscious.

"Mum, this is Tess," Jeremy said.

Mum gave her a warm smile. She didn't seem to notice that she had to look up at Tess instead of down.

"Hi, Tess," Melly Talbot said. "We should have met long before this. I've wanted to thank you for finding

Blue, for one thing. I don't know what we'd have done if you hadn't.''

''Oh, I didn't really do anything. She just came along and I happened to recognize her. If I hadn't spotted her, somebody else would have.''

Although she still looked flustered, Tess was now herself. Jeremy was proud of his mother for having known exactly what to say. But she had not finished yet.

''I should have met you last year when you were in my husband's class. He told me you were one of his most gifted students. Also, of course, I want to know you because you're Jeremy's friend and because I have a hunch you're about to become our new landlady.''

Tess looked slightly overwhelmed. Jeremy didn't blame her. Why did Mum have to go on and on like that? She wasn't as smart as he'd thought.

''I'm glad to meet you, too,'' Tess said politely.

''I had you pictured all wrong, though,'' Melly Talbot said.

Jeremy saw Tess stiffen. He winced inside. Surely his mother wouldn't . . .

''I expected you to be fair like Gwen. I should have guessed that you might resemble your grandfather instead.''

Jeremy breathed again. Tess looked startled.

''I didn't know you knew Gwen . . . my mother, I mean,'' she said huskily. Her glance shifted then from his mother's face to his. He hastened to answer the unspoken question he read there.

''They were together in the hospital. She saw you when you were a baby.''

''I always did wonder what became of the two of you,''

Mum said quietly. "So I was delighted when you turned up in Adrian's class."

Tess smiled. Then she changed the subject.

"Would you like a cup of tea or some hot chocolate?"

"Are we going to have a snack?" Sarah asked, speaking up for the first time in a small but clearly hopeful voice.

"No, we are *not*," her mother said very firmly. "We just had supper, remember? We came over to look at an apartment."

"This way," Mr. Medford said. He went ahead of them but as the Talbots turned to follow him back up the stairs, he called back over his shoulder at Tess, "Put the milk on to heat while we're up there. We can't have this little one going hungry."

They mounted the steps to the first-floor apartment and Mr. Medford unlocked the door and ushered them in. As Jeremy gazed around at the bare, shadowy rooms, he had to fight disappointment. He couldn't see how this shell could ever be a home. Clearly Mum saw things differently. As she chatted with the old man and moved around from doorway to doorway, he could tell that she was picturing the walls newly painted and their furniture all in place. She made no secret of her pleasure in planning. He felt faintly heartened although it still looked like a dump to him.

The three bedrooms were small. But there was one for each of them.

"We can easily double up when we have company," Mum said.

Jeremy glanced at Sarah. She was staring into space as though she did not understand what they were doing there. Then he caught her eye and saw that she, too, was worried. She began to chew the side of her thumb.

When they returned to the basement apartment fifteen minutes later, Tess had hot chocolate and cinnamon toast ready.

Jeremy blew on his cocoa and sipped gingerly. Then, glancing up, he saw that Tess was watching his mother and Sarah. Since there were only four chairs in the Medfords' kitchen, Mum had taken Sarah on her knee. Tess looked wistful.

Jeremy looked away hastily. He sure had some dumb ideas. Tess was no baby. Gwen didn't sound like the kind of mother, though, who would let a kid snuggle up like that. And, if the woman standing next to Mr. Medford in a snapshot taped to the fridge was Mrs. Medford, she looked far too skinny and bony to have made a comfortable lap for such a big little kid as Tess must have been.

"Are we really going to move here?" Sarah asked suddenly, wriggling around so that she could get a clearer view of her mother's face.

"We are," Melly Talbot said, "if the Medfords will have us."

As they were about to leave, while Mr. Medford was saying something to Mum about the lease, Jeremy hung back to whisper hurriedly to Tess.

"She never said a word about knowing your mother till I started telling her what you said. I could hardly believe it!"

Tess seemed to grow distant all at once.

"Did you tell her everything?" she asked in a low voice.

What did she want him not to have spilled? He hadn't

said anything about her clothes. Could that be it? He shook his head, aware of Sarah edging too close for comfort.

''Come on, you two,'' Mum said. Tess gave him a small, tense smile. He hoped it meant things were all right.

But the distance that had come between them that night remained. ''I try to forget her,'' she had said about Gwen. Maybe that was what she was doing now. Maybe she was sorry she had told him so much.

He watched her at school. She still kept apart from the other girls. When everyone else was singing, she didn't join in. At lunch time she mostly read.

Sometimes he wanted to shake her. If she was lonely it was her own fault. How were the kids supposed to know she wasn't a snob when she kept acting like one?

He couldn't help her. He couldn't. He was a boy. The minute he spoke to her at school and let everybody know he liked her, she'd be teased. She'd hate it. So would he.

And Tess knew it, too. If she didn't, wouldn't she come and talk to him in front of the other kids? She must know he wouldn't snub her. He didn't want her to be hurt, that was all. He was only thinking of her.

Twenty-six

The night before the Talbots moved, six o'clock came and there was no sign of supper. Jeremy knew better than to ask his mother when they were going to eat. Next thing he knew, he'd be slaving over a hot stove. He helped himself to a pear.

He had just finished it when Mum came into the kitchen. She had on the old clothes she wore when she was painting. She had pushed the sleeves of her baggy sweatshirt up out of the way but, as he watched, one slipped down. She shoved it up again impatiently. She looked grouchy and tired, as if she'd like to bite somebody. He did his best to fade into the woodwork.

"Hey, Mum, what's for supper?" Sarah asked from the doorway.

That did it.

"What makes you think there's going to be any supper?'' Mum said in a voice so icy that Jeremy felt himself shiver.

That was only the beginning. As she launched into her tirade, Jeremy couldn't help admiring her flashing eyes and the way the long, ferocious sentences came rolling off her tongue. He thanked his lucky stars he had not been such an idiot as to ask about supper, much as he'd wanted to know.

Then, to his own surprise, he found himself actually interrupting her.

''Woman, hold your whisht,'' he said. ''Nobody will have to cook because I'm taking the whole family out for hamburgers. We'll leave as soon as you two can make yourselves presentable.''

Sarah stared at him. His mother gave him a strange look he could remember seeing once or twice before lately. He shifted uneasily under her gaze, hoping she was not about to do something dumb like kiss him or start to cry.

''Whatever you say, Mr. Talbot,'' she said, her voice as soft as when she sang to Sarah. ''I'll hurry but I do need a shower. I feel as if I've spent the entire day grubbing around in King Tut's tomb.''

When she had vanished into the bathroom, Sarah, still staring at him, remarked, ''You sounded like Daddy.''

''I did not,'' he retorted automatically. He hadn't meant to. The words and the tone in which they were spoken had just come to him. Had he heard his father say them? He guessed he had.

''You'd better get cleaned up, too, or you won't get so much as a french fry out of me,'' he growled.

''Where did you get the money?'' she pried.

He had never shown them the money Uncle Ralph

had pressed on him after the funeral. Now he was glad he had kept quiet about it.

"Don't you wish you knew," he said, grinning in a way he knew would infuriate her.

As Sarah went out the door to school the next morning, the movers arrived. Much to Sarah's disgust, both he and Tess were being allowed to stay home from school to help. Mum went to the apartment to show the movers where things should be put as they were carried in. When the house was completely empty, Jeremy followed on foot, locking the door behind him for the last time. He lugged Blue along in a wicker basket with a lid. Blue, yowling with outrage every step of the way, was his biggest worry. What if she didn't like the new place? What if she got out somehow and was lost all over again?

When he got to the apartment and confided his misgivings to Tess, she said she had heard that all you had to do was butter a cat's paws to make it settle down. Mum caught them in the act and groaned.

"That's exactly what I need! Greasy little paw prints all over the freshly shampooed carpets!"

She relented, however, and let them continue, only telling them to shut Blue up in the bathroom when they had finished. A few minutes later they left the small cat contentedly licking her paws. She evidently approved of butter.

Then the two of them began running errands and putting things away. In the middle of the afternoon, Mum loaded them down with sheets and pillowcases and blankets and sent them to make up the beds. As they worked, Tess began to sing softly. Jeremy had never seen her look so happy.

"How come you never sing at school?" he asked.

She stopped abruptly. He could tell by the startled look on her face that she had not even known she was singing until he mentioned it.

"What do you mean?" she asked in a small, tight voice.

"I've seen you," he said, irritated by her stiffness. "When we sing 'O, Canada' in the morning, you just stand there with your mouth shut. Why don't you sing like everyone else? You have a nice voice."

Instead of answering, she snatched up a pillow and swung at him. Two seconds later they were engaged in a battle royal. She had a longer reach but he refused to be daunted. Ducking some of her blows, he did his level best to knock her head off. They erupted into the narrow hall just as one of the moving men was carrying in Mum's jade plant.

The pot shattered on the floor. Tess was appalled. Jeremy was mad at himself. The man swore. Mum only sighed, smiled tiredly and sent Jeremy for the broom and dustpan. He knew it was her favourite plant and she knew he knew.

"Don't look so stricken, Tess," she said. "I'll repot it. It might as well get transplanted along with the rest of us. Maybe a shaking up will do it good."

She turned away. Tess looked at Jeremy, her eyes seeking reassurance. He grinned at her.

"It's no big deal," he said, "but maybe I'd better do the rest of the pillows. Who knows what you might clobber next?"

They did them together. She did not sing.

As they finished, the moving men departed. Jeremy looked around at the chaos and groaned. He'd had no

idea what a horrendous job was lying in wait for him.
The furniture was now in place but nothing else seemed
to be.

"Break time," Mum said, poking her head in at his
door. "I've put the kettle on and I've actually located
both milk and cookies. Come out to the kitchen and join
me."

Tess gave one extra tug to the bedspread, eliminating
an invisible wrinkle, and the two of them followed his
mother. They arrived in time to see her reach to shift a
pile of oddments off one chair. The next second she was
just standing there, her hands full, unable to find a spot
where she could set them down. Jeremy laughed. He
shoved over some of the things on the table to make
room. Then he took his glass of milk and half-a-dozen
cookies and seated himself on the floor. Tess did likewise,
though she took only two cookies. Mum smiled at them
and sank down gratefully on the one chair.

Nobody said a word for the first couple of minutes.
They were all too tired. Tess clearly felt shy, too. Jeremy
hoped she wasn't still worrying about the smashed
flowerpot.

"Tess, there's something I want you to know," his
mother said suddenly. She paused then for an instant,
as if she would like to take it back. They stared at her.
She smiled and went on. "This probably isn't the right
time or place. But we're by ourselves now and I don't
know when that will happen just this way again."

What on earth was she going to say? Jeremy glanced
over at Tess and then looked away hastily. Her eyes were
dark with alarm.

"It's about when you were born," Mum said to her.

"Jeremy tells me you think you weren't wanted and I know that isn't true. I know because I was there."

She looked right at Tess, her eyes understanding.

"Perhaps you would rather I didn't rake it up," she said gently. "I can see how you might feel that way. But from the little Jeremy told me, you have it all wrong."

Tess was sitting bolt upright now. She had her hands gripped around her knees. Jeremy saw that her knuckles were white. She no longer looked alarmed but she did not look happy, either. She appeared braced for whatever was coming.

"Gwen was a child, really," Melly Talbot said. "After all, she was only four or five years older than you are. As a matter of fact, you are far more grown-up right now than she was. She didn't want a baby. It was all arranged that you were to be adopted. She wasn't even going to see you. Then a nurse, who hadn't been told, brought you in to her to be fed, and the minute she held you in her arms, the adoption plans went out the window. She wanted you enough to fight your grandmother. Your grandmother definitely did *not* want you. She had lots of good reasons but mostly, I think, she was ashamed. She wouldn't even look at you. The more she said Gwen must give you up, the more determined Gwen was to keep you."

Tess shook her head. She broke in, her voice hard and cold.

"That's not true. She left me. Grandma was the one who kept me, not Gwen."

"I know she left but that was later, Tess. When she first saw you, she did want you. She wanted you to be hers, to love her and need her. The trouble was that she wasn't old enough or wise enough to be a mother. She wasn't prepared for you to be cranky. She didn't stop to think that you would grow up and have a mind of your own. She wasn't ready to give up her life for you the way your grandmother tried to make her. If she hadn't had to live at home, things might have been different for you both.''

She stopped talking for a moment. Tess sat as if turned to stone. Jeremy took shallow breaths, so as not to break the silence. His mother gave a small sigh and began talking again.

''You were wanted, though, really and truly wanted, by somebody else,'' she said.

''Who?'' demanded Tess harshly. Jeremy could see the scorn in her eyes.

''Your grandfather wanted you always,'' Melly Talbot said gently, her voice sure. ''His face lit up the first moment he saw you and it did again every time he laid eyes on you. I used to go out to the hall so Gwen and your grandmother could be alone. He was always standing at the window of the nursery, smiling in at you. He didn't say much. He didn't get into their argument. But the day I went home, he put an end to it. 'We're taking the baby home,' he said to your grandmother. 'She's our own girl, my granddaughter, and I want her with us. It's settled. She comes home to us.' ''

Tess's face went down against her knees all at once. Jeremy could see her shoulders shaking. He wished he were somewhere, anywhere, else.

He got up abruptly and took his milk glass to the sink. Behind him he heard his mother push back her chair.

''Now it's time we three went back to hard labour,''

she said briskly. Her hand rested for a moment on the girl's dark hair as she spoke.

Jeremy was relieved. He had begun to feel like an eavesdropper. He ran cold water into the glass, turning the tap on full so it made lots of noise.

Tess scrambled to her feet. She held her head high. Her voice was cool.

"Thanks for telling me, Mrs. Talbot. I know you mean to be kind. Gwen didn't want me for long, though, did she? And I've been a burden to my grandparents. Grandpa would never say so but I know. But thanks for trying . . ."

The voice, so certain one moment, wavered then and Tess was silent. Melly Talbot stood looking up at her.

"Poor Gwen," she said then. "She needed a mother herself, you know. She could never have been the mother you should have had. Yet your grandfather loves you more than enough to make up for it. You must know how proud he is of you. When we're alone, what does he talk about? Tess, Tess and more Tess. . . . Now let's unpack these kitchen dishes. You take them out of the box and, Jeremy, you bring them over to me."

She climbed up on a step-stool and stood waiting. Not looking at each other, Jeremy and Tess returned to work.

Twenty-seven

*I*mmensely proud of what they had done, Tess and Jeremy took Sarah on a guided tour. She gazed around forlornly.

"It doesn't look like home," she said in a small, sad voice.

Jeremy was incensed. He knew what she meant, of course, but for him the difference was one of the things that made this a happy place. Here they could make a new beginning.

Tess had departed and the Talbots had finished supper before Sarah discovered Fiona was missing. She had other dolls but Fiona was her special favourite. Everybody joined in the search. At first Jeremy felt sympathetic but soon he got fed up with his sister.

"Fiona, oh, Fiona, where are you?" she kept wailing. Finally he couldn't stand the sight of her, tragic and tear-stained. He had felt terrible when Blue was lost, he remembered, but Blue was alive. That was different.

"Quit whining! If you'd taken proper care of her, she'd be here right now," he told her, his voice rough with impatience. "Anyway, she's just a doll — just a crummy hunk of plastic with hair."

"Take it easy, Jeremy," Mum said. "Sarah was at school all day, remember? You and I were the ones who packed things off."

"Yeah, but she was supposed to put all her stuff to-gether in a box . . ."

"Never mind that now," his mother said sharply. "Keep looking. You're making a bad situation worse."

Jeremy shut his lips tightly and went on turning out the contents of millions of boxes. Fiona did not emerge.

"Maybe Tess saw her," he suggested finally.

Sarah brightened.

"Go and ask her," Mum said.

Tess did not know the doll's whereabouts but she came along to help with the hunt.

It was unbelievable how much stuff had collected. There seemed to be always another box waiting. After awhile Jeremy was convinced he was looking in the same boxes over again. Finally, just when he was telling himself gloomily that he was going to go on doing this for the rest of his life, his mother sank down on a chair and drew Sarah to her.

"Honey, I'm sure Fiona will come to light eventually but we can't keep hunting any longer right now. It's past your bedtime."

"I can't sleep without Fiona," Sarah wept.

"Let's go see if one of your other dolls needs you to help her settle."

Still drooping with sorrow, Sarah let herself be led away.

Except for a few seconds on the stairs, this was the first time Jeremy had been alone with Tess since Mum had spoken to her about Gwen. He groped desperately for words, any words to fill the silence. Then Tess saved him the trouble.

"Your mother is wonderful, isn't she?" she said.

Jeremy, who had been ready to disown that same mother less than an hour before, nodded dumbly.

"She's okay most of the time," he said. "But you've only seen her good side. She's a real dragon when she gets mad. But mostly, she's . . . she's great."

Tess saw through him instantly. She broke out laughing at his sheepish look.

"Who are you trying to kid?" she mocked.

He didn't mind her laughter. At least she was the same old Tess again. Dare he ask her about . . . "Did your grandmother lie to you then about Gwen?" he blurted. "You said . . ."

"I know what I said," Tess frowned, the lightness gone in a flash. At last she spoke, the words coming out slowly.

"She didn't tell out-and-out lies. At least, I don't think she did. Maybe she just didn't know how to talk to kids. I thought . . ."

She broke off abruptly. Jeremy looked away. Why hadn't he let well enough alone?

But her control only faltered for a moment. "That stuff about Grandma and Gwen is no news to me really, you know. What I didn't know was the part about Grandpa choosing to keep me. I guess your mother wouldn't just say that if it wasn't true, would she?"

Her eyes searched Jeremy's face. He looked steadily back. "If she says he wanted you, he wanted you."

"Yeah," Tess said slowly.

An hour later, when they were putting the books on the shelves in Jeremy's room, Mr. Medford knocked on the door of the apartment.

"I dropped by to ask if I could help," they heard him say, "and to make sure Tess isn't getting in the way."

"I'd be lost without her," Mum told him.

Jeremy stole a look at Tess. She was sitting crosslegged on the floor in front of his bookcase, simply smiling into thin air. He bent his head over the paperbacks he was sorting.

A while later, he raised his head again. The hum of conversation coming from the kitchen had suddenly ceased.

"Aren't they awfully quiet out there?" he asked softly.

"I didn't hear Grandpa leave," Tess said, puzzled.

Then Melly Talbot's voice reached them.

"It's not fair. You have this down to a science. I don't stand a chance."

Without a word, Tess and Jeremy jumped up and went to see what was going on. They found the adults sitting down, sipping mugs of coffee and playing Chinese Checkers.

"How did you know he likes Chinese Checkers?" Tess asked.

"I didn't," Mum said. "It was pure luck. I turned up both the board and the marbles during the search for Fiona. Now don't distract me or he'll win."

"He beats me every time," Tess told her.

Sarah, looking angelic in her long white nightgown, came wandering into the kitchen at that moment. She seemed to have forgotten Fiona.

"I'm thirsty," she offered as an excuse.

"You should be sound asleep," Mum said, jumping one of her marbles halfway across the board and looking pleased with herself.

Sarah did not appear to hear this. She gazed at Mr. Medford.

"I don't have a Grandpa," she said, her voice wistful.

Mr. Medford hesitated. "I could pinch-hit for one, maybe."

"What?" Sarah said inelegantly.

"I could be your Grandpa if you like," the old man offered.

Sarah padded over and leaned confidingly against him.

"Your move," her mother said.

Mr. Medford, who had almost all his men in place and who could win in three moves, took up the marble he should have jumped over and moved it in the wrong direction.

"Grandpa . . . !" Tess began in an astonished voice.

"My move," Mum said firmly, quelling her with a steely glance. She no longer looked tired. Jeremy studied the board. His mother had been four moves behind a minute ago. Now things looked even.

"I'd like to have you for a Grandpa," Sarah murmured, snuggling up as though the gruff old man was a jolly, well-loved uncle.

"Well, I guess my girl can share me," he said, putting one arm around her.

"Tess is your girl, isn't she?" Sarah sounded knowing.

Tess's grandfather shot a look at her.

"Yes, Tess is my girl," he told the child now sitting on his lap.

Tess stared at him but Jeremy was the only one who

noticed before she turned her back and went hastily to the sink to get Sarah her drink of water. Then Mum jumped her last marble into the home space.

"I win," she said pleasantly, her eyes gleaming. "Back to bed, Sarah."

Jeremy and Tess burst out laughing. Sarah looked wounded. Mr. Medford sat and stared down at the neat triangle of marbles in stupefaction.

"Well, I'll be!" he muttered and put Sarah off his lap.

After that evening, Tess didn't bring up the subject of her family again. She and Jeremy talked about lots of other things: books, Kim's part in the play, Blue, Mr. Darling. Everything under the sun except her mother — and his dad.

One afternoon, after the two of them had walked home without saying much of anything and he was alone in his own room, he realized that he had been wrong when he had thought she must feel about Gwen the way he did about his father. It was harder for Tess because Gwen had chosen to leave her. He knew his father had not wanted to die.

Then, a week later, Mum found Fiona in a trunk filled with bedding, and Jeremy discovered that Hoot was missing.

Twenty-eight

Jeremy could remember purposely placing the little stone owl behind his dictionary at the back of his desk in his new room, so that he wouldn't have to see it every time he looked up. So when he started to check the correct spelling of ''parallel,'' he noticed right away that Hoot was gone. At first he thought it must have simply been shoved to one side but he quickly realized it was nowhere on his desk. Seeing it all the time had brought back too many hurtful memories but the thought of losing it made him feel slightly sick. He checked through the desk drawers, got down on his knees to search the floor, went over the top of his dresser. No Hoot.

He crossed the hall to Sarah's room. He knew she was there because he had heard Mum giving her a lecture about the mess it was in and sending her to tidy it up.

"Sarah," he said, keeping his tone casual, "do you know where Hoot is?"

Sarah did not seem to have heard him. She was on her hands and knees, picking up dirty socks. He waited a minute. Then he asked again.

This time she shrugged irritably.

"How should I know? If you'd taken proper care of it, you'd have it now."

Much as he longed to give her a good slap, he held onto his temper. He did not want Mum to hear yells from his sister and come to investigate. Sarah would be sure to tell her that he couldn't find his owl. Mum would not say much, but he knew she would mind. Often he had seen her pause while cleaning his room or discussing his schoolwork with him, and pick up Hoot. She would close her hand around it or run her fingers gently over its smooth surface.

He could still hear his father's voice teasing, "You can't have everything, Melly." He was sure she remembered, too, and that was part of what made Hoot special to her.

If she did ask, maybe he could put her off. After all, he did it nearly every day, whenever he could see she was wanting to have a heart-to-heart talk with him. He knew what she wanted to talk about. Dad. She wanted him to remember.

Why couldn't she see that forgetting was better? Talking about Hoot with her would only make them both remember too much.

About a week later when Jeremy came home from school, he discovered that Mr. Medford had put up a bird feeder in the backyard, not far from the Talbots' kitchen window. He had not known before that Mr. Medford cared about birds. His mother and Sarah liked them but they weren't interested in them the way he and Dad were.

Ever since the day Mum had told him that his father was not going to come home from the hospital, Jeremy had avoided looking at birds as much as possible. They seemed so free, so chirpy and lively, so taken up with the details of weather and worms, that they had angered him somehow.

Now, though, with someone to talk to about his discoveries and observations, birdwatching no longer seemed a betrayal.

Dad would want me to keep it up, he started to think. Then he pushed the thought away.

He went inside and found Tess, Sarah and Mr. Medford clustered at the Medfords' back window, watching the birds arriving. Because the house was built on a hill, their rear window also had a good view of the yard. He joined them for a moment, long enough to see a fat blue jay come diving down after the sunflower seeds.

"I'm going to tell Mum," Jeremy said then.

Mum emerged from her book with a weary sigh when he called to her to come and see the surprise. She leaned against the window frame, pleased more by his excitement than by the sight of the growing flock of birds. She looked far more overjoyed when Sarah came running up after him to tell her that all the Talbots were invited to have supper downstairs.

"Grandpa's putting on a big pot of chili. He says he'll send your chili up on a plate if you want to get your paper finished. Tess and I are going to buy ice cream."

"Wonderful!" Mum said. "Bless the man."

Off Sarah went, looking important.

When they were at the table, Mr. Medford said to him, right out of the blue, ''Why don't you call me Grandpa?''

Jeremy looked confused. Sarah had been calling the old man Grandpa ever since they had moved in but he had been unable to follow her example. He glanced around quickly, hoping for a diversion from Sarah or Tess. Sarah looked smug and Tess was grinning.

A fine friend you are, he thought.

Then his glance slid to Mr. Medford himself. Could he be imagining it or did Mr. Medford look nervous?

''Well, cat got your tongue, boy?'' Tess's grandfather barked. ''You go ahead and call me Grandpa the way young Sarah does. Call me whatever you like but stop this everlasting 'Mr. Medford.' Makes me sound like a stranger.''

Jeremy swallowed.

''I'd like to call you Grandpa,'' he said, ignoring the girls.

Mr. Medford smiled at him.

''Try it a couple of times and it'll slip out as slick as a whistle,'' he promised. ''Now take your mother another dish of ice cream. She's too thin.''

Jeremy was glad of an excuse to escape. He raced up the stairs.

''Mr. Medford . . . Grandpa sent you some more ice cream,'' he said to the back of the book she was holding. ''He thinks you're too skinny.''

''If only he were right,'' Melly Talbot murmured.

She was reading and eating simultaneously when Jeremy departed. He managed to say ''Grandpa'' three times before he and Sarah went home.

We're a family, he thought as he sat down to do his

homework. Grandpa and Tess and the three of us. We're a family.

Then, glancing up from his math, he saw the empty space where Hoot should have been. They were not a family. How could they be with Dad not there? He had left an empty space nobody else could fill.

They would never be a whole family again.

Twenty-nine

The next morning Jeremy went to call for Tess. Every day they walked most of the way together, splitting up without comment just before they turned the last corner. He did this for her sake. Surely she could see that.

In the last period they had Music. Miss Mountjoy was starting on the pieces they were going to sing at the school concert in December. She gave them the opening chords for a song they already knew, just to get them warmed up. Then he, and everyone else, heard a new voice. Behind him Tess was actually singing.

The music teacher stopped playing the piano right in the middle of a bar. The class, taken by surprise, kept going a second or two longer. Then the song ended raggedly. They craned their necks to stare, as Miss Mountjoy herself was staring, at the tall girl standing at the back. Miss Mountjoy recovered first.

"Tess Medford, start at the beginning again. The rest of you, keep quiet."

Jeremy had twisted around along with everybody else. Tess was scarlet to the roots of her hair. He faced front again, yanking Merv Reuber around with him. The other boy grinned.

"That your girlfriend? I've seen you with her," he said slyly, the words only loud enough to reach Jeremy's ears through the many whispers around them.

"You've got to be kidding!" Jeremy heard himself answering hotly. Now everybody would start in on them.

Then he saw the scorn on the other boy's face.

"Take it easy, man," Merv said. "She's okay. Your dad liked her."

Jeremy stared. Then his attention jerked back to Tess. She was in trouble. She had missed the chord. He had never seen her look more wretched.

"Miss Mountjoy, may I open the window?" he asked loudly. "It's boiling in here."

Now Miss Mountjoy was staring at him. No wonder. The room was chilly if anything. But it was the only way he'd been able to think of to distract them.

"Perhaps you should remove your extra sweater," Miss Mountjoy said drily.

"Now why didn't I think of that?" he said, making a big production out of getting his sweater off over his head. He was acting like an idiot and he knew it. He heard some of the girls titter. But he'd given Tess a little time.

"All right, Tess," Miss Mountjoy said firmly. "Now that Jeremy is no longer boiling, I want you to sing. I think, from the little I heard, that you have a beautiful voice. For heaven's sake, use it. Right now."

She began to play again, this time leading up to the beginning rather than sounding only one chord. Tess gave a small, husky cough and obeyed. She still looked embarrassed but the notes she sang were true and sweet.

Miss Mountjoy beamed.

"I think you're really an alto," she said. She spoke to the whole class then, but more as if she was talking to herself. "Do you have any idea how much I've longed for a strong alto? Once her voice is trained . . ."

Her words trailed off. The class eyed Tess uncertainly. Jeremy, instead of looking at her, was scanning their faces. Someone snickered. Everyone showed surprise. But only one or two appeared unfriendly.

Had they ignored her just because she ignored them? Were they ready to be friends with her if she made the first move?

He didn't know. The only thing he did know was that she never would make that first move on her own. Never in a million years.

When the bell rang to end the period, Miss Mountjoy spoke to Tess again. They all heard what she said.

"You be at choir rehearsal at three-thirty this afternoon, Tess, or I'll come personally and fetch you."

Jeremy tried not to let anybody see how pleased he was. He'd been right when he'd told Tess she had a nice voice. He knew his mother would be happy when she found out. He wished he didn't also know how tough it was going to be for Tess to walk into the music room all by herself.

The minute the last bell rang, without stopping to think it over in case he lost his nerve, Jeremy marched over to Tess's desk. She was gathering up her books and she didn't notice him for a second. Other people noticed, though. He didn't need to look around to be sure of that.

"Come on, Tess," he said, his words coming out in what sounded to him like a shout, "let's go join the choir."

He'd meant to say more, but at that point his voice, so much too loud the instant before, dried up in his throat. Sure enough, everyone within earshot was staring at them. He stood his ground and waited for what seemed like years.

For Tess was staring, too, her mouth a little open, her grey eyes blank with astonishment. Then she smiled.

"I'm coming. Don't rush me."

As the two of them started down the hall together, he realized suddenly that lots of other kids were hurrying along to the rehearsal, too. Well, no wonder. Miss Mountjoy was great.

He felt so happy in that moment that he thought he might easily float along above the ground if he could just get airborne. After all this time, he had finally stood by Tess and let everyone know he was her friend. And it hadn't been hard, not really. Once he'd gotten those first words out, it had been easy.

Now he recognized that through the weeks he had been telling himself it was up to Tess to make the first move, he had known deep inside that she was waiting for him. She had guessed he was scared that the kids would think he was weird, too. That was why she had never asked it of him, not even with a look. But now he had done it without her asking, and he felt as free as a bird.

Did Dad know? Somehow it felt as if he did.

Thirty

Jeremy tried to keep his voice casual as he told Mum the big news.

"Miss Mountjoy needed more guys in the choir," he said, "so I thought I'd give her a break. Tess joined, too. Miss Mountjoy practically begged her because she's an alto. Tess, I mean, not Miss Mountjoy. We're going to sing in a concert in December."

He heard himself going on and on. Hastily he stuffed his mouth full of bread and butter. Doing his best to chew with his mouth shut, he glanced at his mother.

She was grinning at him. Even though he had quit babbling, she had seen right through his off-handed manner. She was glad for Tess and she was pleased with him.

"Guess what," she said. "Margery phoned this afternoon. She's decided not to go south till January this year. She's coming to spend Christmas with us."

Christmas, Jeremy thought. Panic seized him. Christmas couldn't be coming yet. He stared wordlessly at his
mother.

Sarah was looking at Mum, too. Her expression was
ominous.

"Where will she sleep?" she demanded.

Mum chuckled.

"It will mean doubling up. You'll have to sleep with
me, my sweet."

Sarah's scowl vanished. Jeremy felt better. It wasn't
often that it was an advantage to be the only boy but this
was one of those times. And she wasn't coming for ages.
It was still November, after all.

Snow fell that night, the first snow. When Sarah saw it
the next morning, she ran outside, still in her nightgown
and bare feet, to catch snowflakes in her hands and feel
them falling on her upturned face. She was so excited
that she didn't remember to close the door. She forgot all
about Blue who had been waiting for this chance ever
since the first bird had arrived at the feeder.

The cat slid past her, silently as a shadow. Too late,
Sarah saw. Her scream brought Jeremy racing to the
still-open door. Blue, belly to the ground, was creeping,
step by stealthy step, toward the feeder. Jeremy dashed
out after her but he was one second too late.

Blue's paw snaked out with the speed of light and
batted a chickadee out of the air, sending it spinning.
The other birds took off in a mad flurry of wings. Jeremy
pounced on his cat, grabbing her with hard, clutching
hands, and looked over her head, hoping against hope
that the one tiny bird would fly away like the rest.

It lay where it had fallen. He could see it quivering. Its
eye, the one he could see, blinked shut.

"Fly," he said in a strained whisper. "Fly!"

Its wings stayed folded.

Sarah was right behind him now, crying hard. Jeremy, dodging around her, ran back to the house and thrust the wildly struggling and spitting Blue inside. Slamming the door, he tore back and dropped to his knees beside the small, still bird. Holding his bottom lip between his teeth, he picked the light body up and held it cupped in his palms. His hands felt too rough, too awkward. He could feel its heart beating incredibly quickly. There was no blood, no mark at all to show it had been struck.

"Get Mum," he told his sister, hope strengthening in him.

But Mum came without being called.

"Oh, a chickadee," she said softly, looking but not touching.

"It's alive . . ." Jeremy started to tell her.

As he spoke, the rapid pulse beat weakened, fluttered and ceased. The chickadee's small head dropped sideways against his thumb.

"Don't die," he begged it. He was unaware of Sarah, staring not at the limp bird but into his face, or of his mother putting her arm around his shoulders. "Please, don't die."

"It's dead, Jeremy," Mum said, her voice quiet and matter-of-fact.

He made no answer. Knowing she was right, he still willed the chickadee to live.

Sarah rubbed at her wet cheeks, shivered and said, "Can we have a funeral?"

"Not now," her mother said absently, all her attention fixed on Jeremy. "Hush, Sarah. Go inside."

She opened his hands and took the frail bundle of feathers from him then.

"Come in, son," she said. "You have to eat your breakfast."

Jeremy didn't move. He simply stayed there by the deserted feeder, staring down at the ground.

It wasn't Blue's fault, he thought dully. Blue's a cat, not a person. I'll have to put a bell around her neck.

"Jeremy's not coming!" he heard Sarah reporting.

"He will," Melly Talbot said from the doorway. "Leave him be, Sarah. Go and get some clothes on, for pity's sake."

Jeremy turned toward the house, moving as though in a dream. Snowflakes touched his cheek and melted. He saw one perfect one floating down and then another and another. They were so delicate, like stars.

Then it hit. That little bird was dead. It would never again come to eat the seeds from the feeder. It hadn't been hurting anyone. It had trusted them and Blue had killed it. He had felt death happen in his own two hands and he had been helpless.

His thoughts, going out of control, slid toward his father but he jerked them away with a great effort.

Struggling for mastery of himself, he stopped in his tracks and stared up at the peaceful, luminous sky from which the snowflakes still drifted down, soft, starry white, as beautiful as ever.

"I hate you. I hate you!" he choked.

He did not know to whom he cried out or against whom. Was it God or death? Or was it himself, loving the first snowfall and still alive to see it?

Thirty-one

The next morning more snow fell. After school Tess, Sarah and Jeremy collected enough to make a midget snowman.

"He needs a pipe," Sarah said, surveying him critically.

Jeremy raced inside and came back with a cardboard sign. It said thank you for not smoking. The others laughed as he hung it around the snowman's neck.

When Mum came home, he took her out to see it by the light of a flashlight. She chuckled. Then he heard her breath catch.

"Oh, Jeremy, remember what fun we had dressing that snowman up to look like your dad?"

He flinched.

"We'd better go in," he told her. "Your dinner will be getting cold."

But even though he did his best not to think about his father, he couldn't stop himself. What was it Tess had said about Gwen? "I try to forget her. It's the easiest way." Did she really find it easy? She hadn't spoken about her mother for a long time. Maybe it got easier as you went along. He didn't think about Dad so often now, not since they'd moved.

Mum wanted them to remember, he knew. "As long as we keep your father in our hearts, he will still be alive for us." But he wished that she would try to forget.

Then she brought home an Advent calendar. Tomorrow they could open the first small window in it and there would be another one to open every day until Christmas. The one day Jeremy loved even better than his birthday was coming. It was coming whether he wanted it or not. Sitting at the supper table, watching Sarah examining the calendar excitedly, he knew that he didn't want it. Not without Dad.

Christmas! The very sound of the word brought back one memory after another of his father. Dad inventing his own crazy version of "The Twelve Days of Christmas." Dad handing out the money he had helped them save to buy presents. Dad choosing the impossibly tall tree.

For his father had loved everything about Christmas. Even Mum complained about it. When they were opening their stockings last year, she had said, "I'm surprised you don't climb up on the roof at midnight, Adrian, with sugar cubes for the reindeer." And Dad had come right back at her, his eyes filled with laughter, "Why didn't you suggest that earlier? Next year I'll do it and take you up with me!"

Next year.

"Hey, when are we going to eat?" he demanded. "I'm starving."

When Mum handed him his plate, he leaned over it

and shovelled in the food, slopping gravy on his chin and wiping it off on the back of his wrist instead of on his table napkin. Out of the corner of his eye he caught the look his mother was giving him. If she wanted to yell at him, she could go right ahead. He hoped she would. He was in the mood to yell right back.

But Melly Talbot didn't say a word.

After that, every day seemed full of planning for Christmas. Each morning Sarah opened the next window on the Advent calendar. Each evening she crossed off another day on the ordinary one hanging in the kitchen. Then she counted up how many days were left and went around chanting, "Twenty more days, twenty more days!" The Sunday school was going to have a sleigh ride during the holidays. Miss Mountjoy started the choir singing all the carols Adrian Talbot had loved. Wherever he turned, whatever he did, Jeremy found Christmas waiting.

The Talbots and the Medfords went together to the lot to choose their trees, a small one for Tess and her grandfather, a taller one for Jeremy's family. This year, when he was finding Christmas difficult for the first time in his life, Tess was positively glowing at the thought of it. She had caught some of Sarah's excitement and, he thought, she was happy because their two families planned to celebrate together. He was doing his best not to spoil it for her.

The five of them prowled around the lot, examining the mass of evergreens leaning up against each other.

"Ours can't be as big as other years," Mum reminded them for the third time. "Remember we have to fit it into a smaller space."

Their whole Christmas was going to be like that, Jer-

emy thought. There was no room in their lives now for
the huge joy of their past Christmasses.

"How about this one?" He reached blindly for the tree
nearest to him and yanked it upright.

"Jeremy, it's perfect! How did you ever spot it so
quickly?"

Was Mum making fun of him? He looked at his acci-
dental choice. It couldn't have been straighter. It had no
bare spot. It even had some small cones on it.

"I know a good thing when I see it," he bragged.

As soon as the dishes were done that evening, Mum
said, "Now I'd like the two of you to assist me in creat-
ing some superlative tree ornaments."

Jeremy's heart sank. Each year the Talbots did this but
now he wanted no part of it. He had liked doing it before,
but that was when Dad had been there, admiring whatever they came up with, fashioning ridiculous decorations himself, starting them all singing, making the whole
thing fun.

Mum was busy assembling, in the middle of the big
table, anything and everything that could possibly be
used as part of a tree decoration. Jeremy watched as she
collected pipe cleaners, ribbons, cotton balls, straws, tin-
foil and small remnants of felt. She added tissue paper
and sequins and went in search of yarn. She had Sarah
running hither and thither but she had ignored him.
Had she guessed that he was waiting for the chance to
say he was sorry he couldn't help but he couldn't spare
the time?

He stayed where he was, slouched down in his usual
place at the table, and waited. Now Sarah had seated
herself across from him. She was gazing raptly into space,

lost in dreams of the exquisite ornaments she planned to make. He felt a stab of envy. Everything was simple when you were little. His mother still came and went.

Was he imagining things or had her voice dragged when she was suggesting this crazy outburst of activity? Didn't she want to do it, either?

He moved restlessly on his chair. Then, unable to sit still any longer, he rose and crossed to the window.

Nobody made her do it. She could have bought stuff for the tree. Everyone else did.

"Are you contemplating joining us or are you planning to make your contribution from there?" his mother said.

It was as if she had run the tip of an icicle down his bare back.

She *had* guessed and, boy, was she mad!

"I'm coming," he said meekly. Then he added, "In a minute."

Trying to look purposeful, he peered out the window. The early evening was blue-white with black cut-outs of trees and dark blocks of houses standing out against the new snow. He looked up and saw the first stars through the interlaced tree branches. It was so beautiful that he caught his breath.

Behind him he could feel his mother waiting.

Okay. He'd make one thing. But that would be all. Then he'd say he had homework.

He approached the table where the two of them were hard at it, their faces secret and absorbed. If they were missing him, it sure didn't show. He bumped against the table edge, purely accidentally, as he sat down. They glared.

Three minutes later he had completed his decoration.

It was a tin-foil star. Well, kind of a star. It had only four points and it was decidedly lopsided. But it was silver, wasn't it?

Not looking up, in case he met his mother's eyes, he threaded a wire through one of the points and carried it to the tree. His perfectly okay star was going to be the first decoration. He reached far into the prickly middle and hung it where it could be glimpsed but not examined. Standing back, he decided it wasn't all that bad. And nobody could say he hadn't done his bit.

Keeping his back half-turned, he said as off-handedly as he could, ''Sorry I can't stick around but I have this project due for . . .''

Sarah knocked over the rubber cement. Mum, grabbing at it a split second too late, sent an open package of sequins flying. Half of them landed in the pool of glue and the other half scattered over the shag rug. Melly Talbot stared down at the mess and then, lifting her eyes, looked straight at her son. In that moment, he knew that she, too, was finding the coming of Christmas hard to bear. She not only understood but she shared his anger, the anger that had never quite left him since the chickadee had died. And she, too, would rather not be making festive baubles to hang on a Christmas tree.

''S.O.S.'' she said.

Thirty-two

Jeremy jumped. He had not heard his mother say "S.O.S." like that for a long, long time. It was a signal she and Dad used to tell each other that although they couldn't take time to explain, they needed help urgently. He dropped to his knees, pushed Blue's inquisitive nose out of the way, and started to pick up the thousand spilled sequins. Mum dealt with the rubber cement. When he had retrieved all that he could, he got back up to the table and began to put a cotton ball snowman together.

Now, in some way he didn't understand, he no longer felt trapped. It was going to be a good Christmas after all. And he was going to get through it without ruining things for Sarah or for his mother. All he had to do was go along with Mum's plans and keep busy. That shouldn't be so hard to do.

"I got a note from Margery today. She'll be arriving on Christmas Eve," Mum told them.

"Good," he said, smiling.

"What's good about it?" Sarah muttered.

The other two couldn't help laughing. Then Mum said, her voice extremely firm, "I realize you and Margery had a bit of trouble this summer, but if she doesn't hold it against you, you shouldn't hold it against her. Besides, however you may feel about your aunt, Sarah Jean Talbot, you will bear in mind that she is our guest and you will do all you can to make her welcome."

Sarah looked so squelched that Jeremy took pity on her.

"She'll bring you a present," he reminded her, "and she always gets neat presents."

Sarah brightened instantly.

"I'll get her one, too," she said. Then, catching them exchanging an amused glance, she added magnificently, "Something big."

The next Saturday, when Jeremy took her to do her shopping, Sarah bought Aunt Margery's present first. It was a scratch pad to put beside the phone and it was anything but big. Jeremy eyed it dubiously. It looked cheap. But it was up to Sarah, he supposed.

Then came the really serious part of the expedition, finding a gift for Mum. He trailed after his sister as she went up and down every aisle, searching long and hard.

"Look, Jeremy. This is what she'd like," Sarah cried, holding up something for him to see. It was a tiny golden locket shaped like a heart. Jeremy thought that it was intended for a child. It had "I love you" written across it in letters so small they were almost invisible.

"Great!" he said, feeling closer to her than he had for a long time. "She'll love it."

He started shepherding her toward the check-out counter. But when they were nearly there, Sarah grabbed his arm.

"Jeremy," she cried out, frantic, "my money! It's gone!"

She had had the money in a little change purse inside a bigger bag with a strap that went over her shoulder. When she had reached to open the clasp of the shoulder bag, she had found it already undone and the change purse was missing. He knew that to her it had held a fortune.

He drew her as far out of the stream of noisy, pushing people as he could and stooped down so that he could speak right into her ear.

"How much was in it?" he asked.

"Three dollars and ninety-seven cents!" she sobbed.

The amount was not large but it was not nothing, either. Tears were pouring down her cheeks now. Trying to find Sarah's money was out of the question. If somebody had taken it, the person was long gone and, if it had dropped out of her shoulder purse, there was no way they could ask this milling throng to look for it underfoot.

Patting her shoulder awkwardly with one hand, Jeremy dug into his pocket with the other and got out his wallet. He had a five-dollar bill, two twos and seventy-five cents in coins. It was going to mean giving her practically half of all he owned. He did not let himself sigh as he put the two-dollar bills into her hand.

She gazed up at him, her eyes uncertain.

"It'll take me a long, long time to pay you back," she faltered.

He saw the words rather than heard them. He bent down close to her again.

"It's not a loan," he shouted. "It's an early Christmas present."

She could not seem to stop the flow of tears. He gave her a little shake.

"Quit that," he ordered. "Are you going to buy her the locket or not?"

He grinned down at her as she swiped her coat sleeve across her wet face. When they were out in the crisp December air again, he drew a breath of relief.

"What are you giving Mum?" Sarah asked.

"It's a secret," he put her off.

All he had so far was a scarf. He had planned to spend the rest of his money on flowers. Now he didn't think he had enough left. Well, she had always told them that it was the thought that counted. The scarf was the same blue as her eyes.

Then, fifteen minutes after they got home, he caught Sarah at his desk with her hand out as though she were taking something. He pounced on her and grabbed her by the arm. As he bent it back and began to demand how she dared to touch his things, he discovered that she already had something clutched in her fist.

"I didn't take it!" she cried out, panic in her voice. "Honest. I was just putting it back."

He pried her fingers open and found Hoot.

Jeremy looked from the little stone owl in his hand to his sister's face. He tightened his grip on her wrist.

"Where . . . ?" he began.

He did not finish. She had not been taking it; she had been returning it. He released her. She backed away and would have run from the room if he had not barred her way.

"Where was it?" he demanded.

She could not meet his eyes. Her head drooped so that her voice, when at last it came, was muffled.

"In my dollhouse," she whispered.

"What?"

"It was when Fiona . . ." She stopped and then tried again. "When you said . . ."

The whole thing came clear to him then. That day when he had asked her if she had seen Hoot, she had snapped, "If you had looked after it properly, it wouldn't be lost." Hadn't he himself said those very same words to her the night Fiona was lost? She must have taken Hoot to get even with him. And he must have been mean to her often enough to make her keep it until he had given her the money. What a dopey little kid! Now she was standing there staring at her shoes, ashamed and afraid to explain.

"Thanks," he said, "for bringing it back."

Her head jerked up. She gave him back a watery smile.

"Are you going to tell?" she plucked up enough courage to ask.

He shook his head.

"Forget it," he said magnanimously. Then he moved aside to let her pass. "Now beat it. I've got things to do."

When he was alone, Jeremy sat at his desk and looked down at Hoot nestled in his palm. He had not let himself admit until this minute how much he had missed having it within his reach. He held it for a long time. When he put it down at last, he set it where he would be sure to see it every time he looked up from his homework.

Thirty-three

On Saturday afternoon Jeremy looked up from reading the comics to see Mum settling down to knit. The needles clicked furiously because she was trying to get a sweater for Tess finished in time for her to wear at the concert. Miss Mountjoy had asked Tess to sing a solo.

He knew Mum was also making over some of those weird old dresses. About time Tess stopped looking like a ragbag! But . . . it still wasn't going to be enough. Tess didn't need to look beautiful. She needed to look ordinary.

He found Tess's grandfather in the basement working on a doll's cradle for Sarah. Jeremy sat down next to him, sent up a quick prayer for courage and blurted, "Grandpa, you've got to let Tess wear jeans to school."

It was the beginning of a long speech that came pouring out as if he had rehearsed it. He didn't look the old man in the face while he talked. But he noticed his hands, knotted with arthritis, go suddenly still when he said,

"The other kids laugh at her. They do it behind her back but she knows."

He was running out of steam and feeling extremely nervous when he had a final inspiration.

"My mother wears pants all the time," he ended up.

"I've seen her." The tone in which this was said was not encouraging.

Stumped, Jeremy took some sandpaper and began rubbing at a scrap of wood as though he planned to turn it into a coffee table.

"When I was younger than you," Mr. Medford said slowly, "my mother got me a velvet suit with a lace collar. She made me wear it to church. I hated that rig like poison." He gave a dry chuckle.

"What did you do?"

"Survived," came the terse reply.

He then gave Jeremy the headboard of the cradle to smooth. No further mention was made of Tess's wardrobe.

On the night of the concert, Tess stood tall and proud on stage in her new sweater and a plain skirt. As she sang, each word sounded true and clear.

> When Jesus Christ was four years old,
> The angels brought him toys of gold,
> Which no man ever had bought or sold.
> And yet with these He would not play.
> He made Him small fowl out of clay,
> And blessed them till they flew away;
>   Tu creasti, Domine.

Jeremy, listening, suddenly felt again the tiny body of the chickadee cradled in his own two hands. Without warning, his eyes blurred with tears. He blinked them away, grateful that the auditorium was dark.

> Jesus Christ, Thou Child so wise,
> Bless mine hands and fill mine eyes
> And bring my soul to Paradise.

For an instant Jeremy felt miraculously freed by the haunting little song, or perhaps by the way Tess sang it. It was as if for him, too, the little bird had taken wing.

Then his attention was caught by the sound of Mum, who sat next to him, blowing her nose. Glancing around at her, he saw she, too, had tears in her eyes. But he knew there was no need this time for him to take her hand to comfort her. All she was seeing was Tess standing up there, head high, singing her heart out in front of a large audience. He leaned forward and looked past her. Mr. Medford was getting out his big white handkerchief, too. Jeremy was relieved to see that Sarah, seated between the two adults, was dry-eyed and sleepy.

All the same, he was glad the numbers he had had to take part in were in the first half of the program so that he could join in the burst of applause that followed Tess's song.

Then it was Christmas Eve and Aunt Margery arrived with an enormous stack of presents. As they hung up their stockings, Jeremy felt no sadness. The apartment was too full of people and noise. Even Tess was chattering, her fierce shyness missing for once. Finally the Medfords left and it was time for bed.

The apartment seemed smaller with his aunt in it. Jeremy was thankful he had his room to himself. As he opened his window a crack to let in the crisp, cold air, Mum poked her head in at the door.

"I have one more present to wrap. Can I do it in here since Sarah is in bed with the light out?"

"Sure," Jeremy told her.

He was curious. The gift couldn't be for him or she'd have taken it to Aunt Margery's room. She laughed at his puzzled expression.

"Behold!" she said, dumping two pairs of blue jeans out of a plastic shopping bag onto his bed. He stared at them, still mystified.

"For Tess, silly," she said.

"What'll Grandpa say?" Jeremy breathed, gazing at them in delight.

"He gave me the money to buy them."

The tag on the parcel read FOR MY GIRL, LOVE, GRANDPA.

Mum was standing by his desk now. He saw her fingers go out automatically to scoop up Hoot. He wondered if she had noticed the owl's absence. He thought she must have. He got into bed and watched her gazing down at the small, fat, solemn bird, resting in her open palm. She began to quote softly from *Nicholas Knock*.

> "Ookpik,
>   Ookpik,
> By your
>   Grace,
> Help us
>   Live in
> Our own
>   Space."

She was looking at him from across the room, her eyes serious.

"It's hard, really hard," she mused, putting Hoot down gently, "to live in our own space which is here and now."

He did not know what she was talking about. He lay hoping that she would soon leave.

"Relax, Jeremy," she said with a little laugh. "I know you pretty well by now, you know. I'm not going to make you talk about anything you don't want to talk about. I only want to say that, although this Christmas is different and sometimes very lonely, let's you and I make it a good Christmas for Sarah and Margery and the Medfords."

"Sure," he said. Hadn't he already decided to do just that the night they had made the tree ornaments?

She was coming toward the bed. She'd want to kiss him. Well, why not? It was Christmas Eve.

"I want it to be good for you, too," she said huskily. Then she added in a whisper, "We need each other so much, you and I, now that . . ."

She stopped. He knew why. His face had closed against her. He was sorry but he couldn't help it.

While he was trying to think of something safe to say, she startled him by stooping, kissing him lightly on one ear, and leaving him.

"Goodnight," she said from the hall. "See you at seven and not before."

"Yeah," he called back.

He lay waiting for the tingling excitement that always came when you were in bed on Christmas Eve and knew that when you woke up it would be Christmas morning. This was the magic moment when Christmas really began. Through all the weeks leading up to right now, he had been certain that even without his father, no matter where they moved, whoever was spending Christmas with them, at this very moment a fountain of joy would spring up inside him. It always had. It always would.

He felt no joy. Oh, he was looking forward to opening his gifts. But that was all. He lay dry-eyed, facing the truth that for the first time, it wasn't going to come, not to him, not tonight, maybe never again.

Thirty-four

It was almost morning when he woke up. Four or five o'clock maybe. He wasn't sure how he knew. He just did. And it was Christmas.

He couldn't wake Sarah because she was in with Mum. Yet he knew he couldn't go back to sleep, either. He peered over the edge of his covers at Blue.

"Merry Christmas, cat," he said.

If she heard him, she gave no sign. Not even a whisker moved. He poked her gently. She opened her blue eyes a slit, yawned, covered her face with one paw and refused to wake up.

"What I need is some food," Jeremy said, as if his cat were listening. He tiptoed out to the kitchen, nobly not letting himself so much as glance into the living room where the presents waited. He got himself a banana. When he eased open the door of the refrigerator so that he could pour himself a glass of milk, he heard Blue thump to the floor and come running.

"You're disgusting," he said to her softly. "You won't even say 'Merry Christmas' without a bribe."

Blue polished off the last drop of milk, looked up to see if he had anything further to contribute, accepted the fact that he had not and, turning her back on him, stalked off into the living room. He knew what she was after. She took every chance to go and sit in front of the tree and play with the decorations on the low branches. What she had not broken, they had long since moved up out of her reach, but she still had high hopes.

"No, Blue!" he called after her in a stage whisper. "Come on out of there."

He glanced at the clock on the stove. It was twenty to six. He definitely was not supposed to go near the presents but he had to get Blue, didn't he? She might do some damage.

Blue, to his surprise, was not under the tree but curled up in the big armchair Mr. Medford liked best. Maybe when the lights were not switched on, the tree lost its appeal for her. He left her where she was and turned to look at the row of stockings.

Sarah's was fat and knobbly and so were Aunt Margery's, Tess's and Mr. Medford's. He kept his eyes averted from his own but he couldn't help putting his hand out to feel it. He snatched his fingers away as he recognized the shape of the special pen he had asked for that wrote in six different colours. He grinned. Then he saw that Mum's stocking, which was next to his, was half empty.

He lifted it to be sure he was right. There was a candy cane hooked over the top, but despite that cheerful note, it hung limply. He peered in and saw one mandarin orange and a Christmas cracker. Why hadn't she filled her own?

Jeremy sat down on the couch, pulled the afghan there around his shivering body, and thought. It was the kind of thinking he had not let himself do for a long time. But now there was no stopping it.

Clearly, as if it were happening right now instead of last year and all the years before that, he saw his parents laughing as they dug into their Christmas stockings. They had acted every bit as silly and excited as he and Sarah.

"They didn't know what was in theirs, either," he said aloud. "They never knew what they'd find next any more than we did."

Last year his father had got a paperback murder mystery, some play money "to help with the mortgage," a rubber spider, a chocolate cigar . . . and a little book saying how many calories were in everything. And Mum had had some pills with a poem about how sorry Santa was that she had to live with "three pains in the neck." There had been a small bottle of perfume and a little wooden animal with pink fuzzy hair . . .

Jeremy did not remember what else. He did not need to. He had just figured out something that had been obvious for years but that he had never before realized. Each of his parents had filled the other's stockings.

It must have been fun for them, he thought.

Pain closed in on him as he lived back in those other Christmasses and saw, really saw, what fun it had been. This time he did not push the pain away.

In the next hour, he was sure, over and over again, that he would waken them all and get caught. First he

replaced the skimpy little sock she had hung up for herself with one of his own, one of the socks he wore over
all the others when he went skating. Then he found a
fifty-cent piece he had saved in a little box in his desk. He
added an apple. That helped. Yet he knew there had to
be more.

The scarf he had bought for her! He fetched it from his
bottom dresser drawer. He had wrapped it just in tissue
paper so it squashed up small enough to go in.

Now something funny.

He stood there, worried about the minutes ticking by,
unable to think. He hadn't a single funny thing. Not
one . . . Then he had an inspiration. George! George
was a tiny plastic frog he had got out of a bubble gum
machine. He couldn't find him right away but then he
remembered. He dug his old cords out of the bottom of
the dirty clothes hamper. George was in the left pocket.

There. He stood back and looked. He wished he could
write a poem the way his father had but he was lousy
at poems. Still her stocking did look beautifully lumpy
now.

She hadn't even bothered to put her name on the one
she had hung for herself, although she had made sure
the rest had labels. He printed her name, ''Melly,'' on a
sheet of paper from the telephone scratch pad and pinned
it on. Now hers looked just like the others.

He had done it! Yet he went on standing there. It needed
one more thing, something special, something . . .

Really he knew what it needed. He was trying not to
say it to himself, trying not to give in to his own knowledge.

Hoot. That was what she would love.

But Hoot was his.

"She wouldn't want me to give it up," Jeremy told himself.

He knew better. Didn't her hand go out to it every time she passed his desk? Maybe it was because the owl was so small and yet so unexpectedly heavy. Maybe it was simply because she remembered.

Jeremy went to his room and brought it back. Standing there, the smooth roundness of it still in his hand, still belonging to him, he remembered, too.

"You can't have everything, Melly," Dad had said, smiling. "Hoot is for Jeremy."

It wasn't as if the owl was his only gift from Dad. He had other special things. The copy of *Kim*, for one. And Blue, of course!

And Tess, he thought with a grin.

He went to the telephone table again and got another sheet of paper. Then he saw it was really getting light outside and he hurried. He didn't wonder if Mum would remember, too. He knew she would.

"You can't have everything, Mum," he wrote, "but you can have Hoot. Merry Christmas. Love, Jeremy."

He taped the piece of paper onto the little owl. He stroked it once more and slipped it in quickly. There. It was done.

He wrapped his arms around his body because the furnace had not come on yet and the air was cold. He felt different.

The joy he had so longed for the night before had come. And yet this was a more difficult joy than he had known other years. It was so real, so wonderful, that he felt almost afraid. He stood very still, looking back to the man he no longer wanted to forget, looking ahead to this Christmas which was now, at last, fully his.

What time was it? It didn't matter. He could not bear to wait another second. He wanted them, his whole family. Not even glancing at the clock, Jeremy flew to wake them.

Also by Jean Little . . .

LOST AND FOUND

When Lucy's family moves to a new town, she wonders
if she'll ever make new friends. Then, on her way
home from her first trip to the local store, she meets
a little dog that is friendly and may — or may not —
be a stray. Against her own best wishes, Lucy begins
to hope that the dog has no owner, and that her parents
will let her keep it. But they insist that she make every
effort to find the original owner before letting her
keep the dog. A heart-warming story about loneliness
and love, and the healing relationship between a young
girl and a pet.